I called Mrs. Crofts, just in case she had called the police. I don't like being pursued by cops.

She shouted over the telephone. "Where are you, Martin J.?"

"It's a long address. I'll mail it to you."

"What telephone number?"

I said I could not hear her over the static.

"What static?"

We shouted back and forth until the telephone disconnected. Then I turned to the clerk behind the counter. "What's the name of this town, anyway?"

"Red Rock," he said.

"Red Rock?"

"Red Rock, Idaho." He looked at me suspiciously.

"Red Rock, already?"

D0775701

TEN MILES FROM WINNEMUCCA

THELMA HATCH WYSS

HarperTrophy®
An Imprint of HarperCollinsPublishers

Harper Trophy® is a registered trademark of
HarperCollins Publishers Inc.

Ten Miles from Winnemucca
Copyright © 2002 by Thelma Hatch Wyss
All rights reserved. No part of this book may be used or
reproduced in any manner whatsoever without written permission
except in the case of brief quotations embodied in critical articles
and reviews. Printed in the United States of America. For
information address HarperCollins Children's Books,
a division of HarperCollins Publishers,
1350 Avenue of the Americas, New York, NY 10019.

Library of Congress Cataloging-in-Publication Data
Wyss, Thelma Hatch.
Ten miles from Winnemucca / by Thelma Hatch Wyss.
p.   cm.
Summary: When his mother and her new husband take off on a
long honeymoon and his new stepbrother throws his belongings
out the window, sixteen-year-old Martin J. Miller takes off in his
Jeep and settles in Red Rock, Idaho, where he finds a job, enrolls
in school, and suffers from loneliness.
ISBN 0-06-029783-2 — ISBN 0-06-029784-0 (lib. bdg.)
ISBN 0-06-447334-1 (pbk.)
[1. Runaways—Fiction. 2. Homeless persons—Fiction. 3. Self-
reliance—Fiction. 4. Loneliness—Fiction. 5. Stepfamilies—
Fiction.] I. Title.
PZ7.W998 Te 2002   2001024602
[Fic]—dc21   CIP
                                                                    AC

Typography by Larissa Lawrynenko
◆
First Harper Trophy edition, 2003
Visit us on the World Wide Web!
www.harperteen.com

For Jacob Wilder

1

If I were Walt Whitman I would sling words across this page with such barbaric yelping the corners would curl up. Great clamorous words that tell how it is to be hungry, homeless, and sweating, driving down a glaring freeway south of Seattle in an old red Jeep low on gas with my mountain bike on top and all my other belongings smashed in the backseat.

I would spew out the bitter words of my fury until vengeance was mine on Burgess, my stringy-haired stepbrother of four days:

The smoke of my anger,
The sweat of my soul,
I sound my barbaric yelp down the
  metallic freeway
In an old red Jeep
Low on gas.

But of course, I am not Walt Whitman. He is dead and in his mausoleum in New Jersey with the granite door left partially open at his request, according to Miss Addison, my sophomore English teacher who knows things like that about poets.

I am Martin J. Miller—hungry, homeless, and sweating at age sixteen. But I am alive. And I do not know how old dead Walt entered here, except I turned on the radio to get my mind off Burgess and I heard this song:

You've got to walk that lonesome valley,
You've got to walk it by yourself.
No one else will walk it for you,
You've got to walk it by yourself.

2

The song reminded me of old Walt. He said the same thing over a hundred years ago. I suppose other poets have said the same thing also, in their own ways, but I would not know because I am not a poet. I am more into *National Geographic*.

My friend Pete and I read those magazines every day while we ate our sack lunches at Winnemucca High School, and before that at Winnemucca Junior High, and before that at Winnemucca Elementary. We learned a lot, Pete and I, during lunch.

After school we rode our bikes out over the desert, pulling wheelies and laughing like maniacs. Then we headed for the Red Bandanna on Main Street where we sat in the back booth memorizing Walt Whitman for Miss Addison.

On the last day of school last spring, we had to recite fifty lines from an American poet, individually, before she would give us our report cards. Pete and I thought Miss Addison looked like a little wind-up bird twittering rhymes, but we memorized for her all year because both our mothers are teachers and members of the Ladies Literary Club with Miss Addison.

Pete and I spat out old Walt with great flourish, line after line:

> *Not I, not anyone else can travel that*
> *road for you,*
> *You must travel it for yourself.*

I did not know last spring that I would be going anywhere, that I would be driving that road by myself with one eye on the gas gauge, the other looking for a cheap gas station, knowing if I did not find one soon, I would be walking it for certain.

So when I heard that song on the radio, I naturally thought of good old dead Walt Whitman. Pete and Miss Addison. And Winnemucca, Nevada, where I had lived for sixteen years just off Main Street with Mom Miller. With no complaints. I turned off the radio before the song ended, but it was too late. I was remembering Winnemucca.

The town has two billboards, one at each end of Main Street, erected by the Chamber of Commerce. One side reads:

**WELCOME TO
WINNEMUCCA
ONE TRAFFIC JAM
A DECADE**

And the other side reads:

**COME AGAIN TO
WINNEMUCCA
ONE TRAFFIC JAM
A DECADE**

In between are the Red Bandanna and Olsen's Bakery. And a string of establishments that, according to Miss Addison, cannot spell *and*: Pump 'n' Save, Cut 'n' Curl, and Gas 'n' Goodies.

That's about it, except the cemetery at the west end of town where my father is buried. It has no grass. But we kept flowers on Dad's grave all year: fresh ones on Memorial Day, his June birthday, Christmas, and Easter. The rest of the time we used plastic flowers, as almost everyone else did.

Even without grass it is a nice cemetery, and it makes the west end of Winnemucca look respectable and colorful. So lack of grass in the cemetery is not a complaint of mine, just a description.

I was five years old when my dad died. Since then Mom Miller and I have spent a lot of time in that cemetery on Saturday afternoons, talking to my dad and talking to each other.

Just across from Dad is Maxwell Smith, a boy who died the same year I was born. In addition to flowers, his parents brought real gifts to him: baskets of Easter eggs, jack-o'-lanterns filled with candy, and helium balloons on his birthday. Once they brought a birthday cake with red candles on top. They lit the candles, sang "Happy Birthday," and then cut the cake.

I wanted a piece of that cake so much I told Mom Miller I wished I were that dead Smith boy. She grabbed my hand and we ran out of that cemetery down Main Street to Olsen's Bakery without stopping once for breath.

After that she made certain that on our way home from the cemetery we stopped for a root beer at the Red Bandanna or a cinnamon bun at Olsen's. Also she made certain that I always had gifts of the season. They never did look as spectacular on our kitchen table, however, as they did in the cemetery.

But Mom Miller took good care of me, and I told that to Dad one Saturday—right in front of her. It made her smile.

I had no complaints until last summer when Mom Miller met Mr. Joe Wonderful in Reno. She and Pete's mother drove there each week to the university for teacher recertification, as they did every few summers. In past years she always came home normal: certified, contented, and cooking well-balanced meals for us.

But this summer she met Mr. Joe Wonderful driving around Reno in a white Cadillac, down from Seattle, Washington, to the car auctions. When she came home each weekend she asked me ludicrous questions, apparently heard first from Mr. Joe.

"Don't you find Winnemucca a lonely place, Marty?"

I looked at her in surprise. "No, Mom," I said. "We have never been lonely here."

And the next weekend: "Nevada doesn't get any smaller, does it, Marty?"

"No, Mom," I answered. "We don't want it to."

Mr. Joe Wonderful just kept driving around Reno in his Cadillac asking his questions until Mom Miller could not keep her mind on recertification or the roast drying out in the oven.

And before the summer was over I was pulling out of Winnemucca permanently in my old red Jeep with my mountain bike on top, following his big Cadillac, looking back at the billboard like any tourist pulling out of town.

I followed his Cadillac all the way to Seattle, Washington—where, Mr. Joe Wonderful said, grass grows. Before leaving Winnemucca he had suggested that I sell my Jeep and fly to Seattle. So I drove it all the way. My Jeep and I stick together.

In return for all his absurd questions about Nevada, I had one for him at the wedding. I looked around the chapel at the display of white calla lilies and at the enormous bouquet in my mother's arms, and I wondered how all those fresh flowers would look on my dad's grave. But then I saw my mother's smile and I did not ask.

Mr. Joe Wonderful is rich. He lives in a two-story redbrick Georgian house on upper Ivy Cliff Drive. And he collects coffee tables. I counted six just walking from the front door to the patio where we sat poolside on white-cushioned wicker chairs around more coffee tables. Apparently we were ushered there to enjoy the coffee tables, because no one mentioned going for a swim. They all had glass tops, making it mandatory to notice them unless you wanted to lose a leg.

The first one I noticed had a brass dolphin coming up through it. The dolphin's tail formed the base and his head stuck up above the glass top. He looked surprised that he had come up through a coffee table instead of the swimming pool.

Then there was a brass bear cub on his back, holding up a glass top with four chubby legs. Did he ever look stupid.

The one I almost lost my leg on was an oval bronzed mirror balanced on the knees of an ebony nude girl, her head resting on the mirror, her arms encircling it. She was there for life, sitting on a prickly sisal rug.

When Mr. Joe Wonderful and Mom Miller

left for their honeymoon to Europe, they both waved from the boarding gate. Mom Miller did not seem to notice how old Mr. Joe looked with tufts of gray hair blown awry and his suit jacket stretched over his stomach. She just kept smiling. Mr. Joe shouted to me, "I'll bring you home something nice, Martin J. Count on it."

What I could count on, I imagined, was a glass-top coffee table with half a gondola pushing through.

"Don't bother," I shouted back. "I don't need one."

Mr. Joe Wonderful has Burgess—sixteen years old and big—who thinks he owns the second floor of his father's house. At least that's where he threw all my belongings from, a second-floor bedroom window at the front of the house.

The day before the wedding Mr. Joe's housekeeper, Mrs. Crofts, took me to that bedroom on the second floor and said it was for me, view of Puget Sound included. Four days after the wedding, on Mrs. Crofts's day off, of course, all my things came flying out of that bedroom window in a wild explosion of shapes and colors.

My clothes, all my belongings, landed below the window in the boxwood hedges and holly bushes. My sleeping bag bounced from the hedge and rolled across the grass. My socks flapped from topiary trees. Camping gear, bike helmet, cowboy boots—my life in the bushes.

"Hey," I yelled. "What's going on?" I looked up to my bedroom window where Burgess and his friends were looking down. Sneering.

I had thought Burgess with his stringy hair and constant sneer was one of a kind. But his three friends looked just the same, a quartet of sneering, long-haired bandits.

They leaned over the window ledge and emptied cans of beer down over my things. Then Burgess pulled down the window shade. Scrawled across it in bold black letters was the message: **GET LOST, KID.**

I stood looking up at that window with a hatred I had never felt before. I grabbed all my things scattered around in the bushes and shoved them into my Jeep. I sat in the front seat gripping the steering wheel, barely breathing, until finally I realized that everything I owned was with me. Everything I owned was here in my old red Jeep.

I did not stick around upper Ivy Cliff Drive.

2

All day I followed the freeway, weaving south toward Nevada. I ate hot dogs at gas stops. I was low on cash. Mrs. Crofts had been placed in charge of finances during the three-month honeymoon trip, but with each mile she was receding farther and farther into the distance.

Hot dogs were okay with me. I did not want any help from Seattle. I would go back to Winnemucca, where anyone in town would take me in.

I kept glancing at the rearview mirror expecting to see Mrs. Crofts in a patrol car,

14

her long arm pointing me out: Martin J. Miller, the runaway. Or worse—I expected to see Burgess and his cohorts riding after me on their motorcycles, their noses covered with red bandannas. Shooting at my tires.

No one was following, although once I thought I saw white-haired old Walt over my shoulder, reminding me that I was traveling this road all by myself.

I followed the freeway out of Washington, through Oregon and into Idaho, where I ran out of gas and money. I pulled off the freeway and coasted into a gas station. And I called Mrs. Crofts, just in case she had called the police. I don't like being pursued by cops.

She shouted over the telephone. "Where are you, Martin J.?" She said she was just about to call the police and next time she would.

I said that next time I would leave a note.

She continued shouting. "Are you in Winnemucca?"

"Not yet," I said.

"Burgess said you packed up and went home."

"Burgess doesn't know anything."

"Where are you then?"

"It's a long address. I'll mail it to you."

"What telephone number?"

I said I could not hear her over the static.

"What static?"

"I can't hear you, Mrs. Crofts."

"I can hear you very well, Martin J."

We shouted back and forth until the telephone disconnected. Then I turned to the clerk behind the counter. "What's the name of this town, anyway?"

"Red Rock," he said.

"Red Rock?"

"Red Rock, Idaho." He looked at me suspiciously.

"Red Rock, already?" I raised my eyebrows.

I spent five dollars on gas and I had another five in my wallet. I stared at it awhile and then bought another hot dog. I sat in my

16

Jeep seeing how long I could make a hot dog last and wondering how long I could last in Red Rock, Idaho.

I drove to the center of town, then a few blocks toward the mountains. Ahead on the right I saw a shady park and I pulled in.

It felt good driving under the shade of trees, but to not waste gas I pulled up beside a small pond and parked. I noticed scattered groups of people sharing picnics on the grass. The sight of people eating made me ravenous, even though I had just finished the hot dog.

I remembered passing a hamburger shop a few blocks back and I walked to it and ordered a hamburger with extra pickles. I took it back to the park and sat down on a bench by the pond. I nibbled slowly, seeing how long a hamburger could last.

As I ate, I watched the ducks on the pond swimming around. They stretched their necks and tipped bottom-up in the water, searching for their dinners.

A cluster swam over to the bank, some

with bright green heads, the others brown, and they bounced out of the water and waddled up to me. Quacking and quacking.

"Are you trying to tell me something?" I asked. "Run, run? Stay, stay?" I had never talked to ducks before.

"You are cool little critters," I said, and tossed them a small piece of bread. Someday I would offer more.

"Real cool little critters," I said again. "Don't you think so, Walt?"

I glanced over my shoulder. No Walt. I was all alone. So I stood on the park bench and soliloquized:

The green-necked ducks quacking their song,
The dun-colored ducks quacking their song;
Miracles, these green, these brown ducks,
Quacking their songs.

I sat back down on the bench and watched the ducks until it was too dark to see them. And I decided I would not run back to

Winnemucca. Anyone in town would take me in, but the very next day Pete's mom or Miss Addison would be on the phone calling Seattle.

And I would not run back to the house on Ivy Cliff Drive, either. Until—well—at least until I was bigger than Burgess. I would stay here in this park in Red Rock, Idaho—with the ducks.

I said good night, climbed into my Jeep, and curled up in my sleeping bag on top of my things in the backseat. And tried to sleep.

I had never slept in a public park alone before. In a strange town. I pulled the sleeping bag up over my head.

All night long I heard those crazy ducks quacking in my dreams.

3

I awoke to an earthquake. The Jeep was rocking back and forth, and my head was bumping against the side. The ducks were quacking like crazy. I threw back my sleeping bag and grabbed the front seat.

I don't like earthquakes. Not that I have ever experienced one before. But I have read in *National Geographic* how the earth opens up and swallows people in cars on their way to work or sleeping in a park, never to be heard of again.

I would want to be heard of again. Mrs.

Crofts would never be able to identify me, however, even if she watched the disaster on national news, even if the handlebars of my bike appeared above the crevice. There are hundreds of handlebars just like mine.

I stared through the windshield into the pale gray morning and my eyes focused on two baggy trouser legs swaying on the hood of my Jeep. Someone was standing on my Jeep trying to steal my mountain bike.

I climbed into the front seat, rapped on the windshield, and yelled just like Burgess. "Hey, you. Get lost!"

I rolled down the window a crack and yelled again. "Beat it!"

The man slid down the hood and turned toward me. Just as I rolled up the window, he pressed his lean, whiskered face against the glass.

For an instant, I looked into the man's watery blue eyes and I saw my own face reflected. We both had slept in Homeless Park, so what was the difference between

Baggy Legs and me—Martin J. Miller? For one thing, I decided quickly, he was on the outside pounding on my window, and I was on the inside starting the engine.

"Turn over, turn over," I whispered. It did, and I pressed on the gas pedal and took off. Baggy Legs ran after me, shouting and cursing, until I was out of the park, and then he stood alone in the street, flapping his arms.

I drove toward the mountains for several blocks and then pulled over to the side of the street to think. Without my Jeep there would be no difference between me and Baggy Legs. No difference at all. I loved my Jeep.

I decided to check my bike, just in case. I got out and looked it over. It was still secure in its rack with a cable running through it. I got back inside the Jeep and locked the doors, trying to think logically as my dad would have done. Engineers think logically. They don't panic. And I am just like my dad.

I began a list in my head:

Jeep. The Jeep is the most important thing in the world.

Food. Food is the most important thing in the world.

Shower. A shower each morning is vital.

Graduation from high school is essential.

A subscription to NATIONAL GEOGRAPHIC would be nice.

Who did I think I was talking to? Santa Claus? My dad in the cemetery? I leaned my head on the steering wheel and groaned.

All those cemetery conversations with Mom Miller began rushing back through my head, about my dad not wanting to leave me. It was cancer that took him away. I must understand that. But Mom Miller would be both mother and father. She would never leave me alone—hungry and homeless.

So where was she now?

I pounded the steering wheel with my fists and shouted obscene words to nobody until I was hoarse. Then I just sat and stared at the shadowy mountains, so close I thought they might fall over on me.

After a while the sky became light, although the sun had not yet made it over the tall ragged peaks. I looked around at the quiet street where I had parked. No one was waiting in line to give me any help. So I started the Jeep and drove aimlessly for a few blocks. Feeling low. Way low.

The Burger Box on the corner of 10th South and Harris nearly knocked my eyes out. It looked like a red-and-white checked box waiting for a bus. A sign on top of a red-and-white pole read: BURGERS SO GOOD THEY MAKE YOUR TONGUE WANNA BEAT YOUR FACE.

Usually I would drive right past a cute sign like that, but I noticed a smaller sign in the window: HELP WANTED. I felt better just seeing the sign. I could help for cash. Then I could eat. Buy gas. Be normal.

I pulled into the empty parking lot and waited. About the same time the sun made it up over the mountains, almost blinding me, two men pulled up and went inside. I waited a few more minutes, then went inside to the rest room and splashed water on my face.

I approached the younger man at the counter and told him I had seen his sign in the window.

"Student?" He sized me up pretty well.

"Yes." I nodded. I have always been a student.

"Can you work after school? That's our busiest time."

"I can work after school every day." I tried not to sound too eager. "And on Saturdays also."

"Are you paying for the Jeep?"

"No," I answered. "It's all paid for." Thanks to Mom Miller.

"Mountain bike?"

"Paid for." I guess I am not an only child for nothing.

As he looked me over I wondered how desperate I looked. On the outside I was normal: a short skinny teenager in faded jeans, T-shirt, and cowboy boots. With blue eyes and wavy brown hair. A good-looking, all-American teenager. Well, the nose is longer—my dad's nose.

But on the inside I was Help Wanted. I pushed my hands into my pockets and shifted my boots.

"What about three hours after school each day and three on Saturdays?" he asked.

My mouth fell open. He had just hired me. He had given me a job. I wanted to hug him, swing him around by his arms. "G-great," I stuttered.

"Start tomorrow?"

"I can start today," I said. "After school."

He nodded. "It is minimum wage. We pay every two weeks. Do you have a Social Security number?"

I nodded and then my jaw began twitching. Was he going to ask for an address? A telephone number?

He called to the older man. "Bring a card, Dad. A new employee." He reached out his hand. "I go by Tom," he said. "Tom Flandro. And my dad goes by Mr. Flandro."

I sat in a booth and filled out the card, making up things like a regular con man.

"My address is temporary," I said. "My mom and I are staying with relatives until we find a house. The telephone number is temporary, too."

"Just so I get your Social Security number," Tom said. "You show up for work each day, and I won't be calling you at home."

"Okay," I murmured.

He looked briefly at the card. "You go to Woodland High?"

I nodded. "That's the one. I'm headed there now." I'm always headed for school.

"It's our only one," Mr. Flandro said, smiling. He held out a hamburger on a sheet of red-and-white checked paper that matched the outside paint job. The burger was still sizzling. "Here, try this," he said. "Burgers so good they make your tongue—"

I choked a bit. Ordinarily the metaphor

itself would have killed my appetite. But this was not ordinary. "I just had breakfast," I said. "But, what the heck. I always have room for a burger." I snatched it from his hand.

"Also"—Mr. Flandro chuckled—"we have fringe benefits. All the cold hamburgers you can eat."

"Oh, yeah?" I backed toward the door. "Thanks. See you after school."

Where there is a red-and-white checked Burger Box there is a school nearby, and it did not take me long to find Woodland High. It was only four blocks away, almost hidden by tall pine trees.

The school was a two-story gray stone building with a parking lot in front. Paper posters stretched across the windows: WE LOVE YOU, RAMS! and THE CHOICE FOR ME IS DRUG-FREE. It looked a lot like the school in Seattle where I had just registered, except older and smaller. It was sort of medium, like the town.

For a while I just sat and looked. I felt

guilty being on the outside of a school when I should have been inside, as I suppose all children of schoolteachers feel. When a bell rings, we know where we belong and it is not outside in a parking lot.

I don't like feeling guilty. And so before any bells rang, I turned my Jeep around and headed toward the mountains.

I felt so good having a job I decided I could stay in Red Rock—heck, maybe forever. I could sleep in my Jeep and eat cold hamburgers, and go to Woodland High. I would show Seattle. Of course, when I became an engineer I would go back to Winnemucca. And maybe before.

I had a problem, but now I also had a plan. A good plan. I felt like Martin J. Miller again.

4

I needed a campsite, a safe distance from Baggy Legs. I drove along Foothill Road and saw a sign pointing to Little Red Rock Canyon. A smaller sign below read: NO OVERNIGHT CAMPING. Still, I turned up the narrow road. Every so often I passed a picnic spot, tucked away in the scrub oak and quaking aspen, identified by a paper plate tacked to a tree. Messages left over from summer parties, I supposed. I stopped to look at a few places but decided against them. I needed a private room.

About five miles up the canyon I noticed a turnaround space on the side of the road. I pulled over and looked around. An overgrown trail led into the trees, perhaps going down to a creek, which I could hear in the distance. But the access was blocked by rocks.

Behind the scrub oak I found a secluded spot just the size for hiding a Jeep. I rearranged the rocks—boulders, really—and worked up a good sweat.

Then I drove the Jeep headlong into the scrub oak until it stopped. I climbed out and tried to untangle it. I broke off bushes and small tree limbs and, hacking away with a knife from my tool kit, made a kind of portable gate. From the road, things looked just the same as before, except for the mountain bike perched on top of the bushes. I would park it under a pine tree.

I cleared a space around the Jeep, picking up sharp rocks and broken tree limbs and smashing down what I could not pick up. I felt like a moose trampling down a forest.

Pete and I had a Moose Club when we were in elementary school. We were the sole members. We scheduled meetings, gave a few Moose calls, and then dismissed. Then we walked down to the Red Bandanna and had a root beer.

We belonged to an exclusive brotherhood, Pete and I. Moosehood, we called it. All the boys at school wanted to join, but we always said sorry, the membership was filled. Anyway, I thought about it as I trampled around in the brush. I tried saying "moose" a time or two, but the word caught in my throat.

Occasionally I heard a car pass, but no one stopped. I heard the creek down in the ravine and was glad to know it was there, but I would investigate it later. I squeezed into the Jeep and pulled off my boots and looked around.

For the first time in a long while I felt like smiling. I had found a job and I had found a camp, which I hoped I could find again. I did not want to write my name on a paper plate and tack it to a tree for all the world to see.

I would give my camp a name, a deserving name. But until I thought of one, I would call it A Darn Good Camp.

In the afternoon I rode my mountain bike down to work. I took a change of clothes, rolled up in my backpack. It felt good to be pedaling down a canyon to a job.

But I had no intention of starting the first day of my new job looking and smelling as if I had just pedaled down a canyon. I rode directly to Woodland High, parked my bike in a rack near the front door, and walked in just as the two-thirty bell rang.

Immediately students crowded the halls and I could not see where I wanted to go. Finally I found the basement stairs and then the boys' locker room. I could hear the football team practicing outside and I knew I had the showers to myself. I did not linger, however, and was out before anyone came in.

I smelled great.

I rode my bike over to the Burger Box and arrived fifteen minutes early. The parking lot smelled great, too, like a big greasy hamburger. I wondered how I could endure the tantalizing aroma for three hours.

Mr. Flandro motioned me around the counter and handed me a red-and-white checked apron just like the hamburger wrap and the walls. "How was school?" he asked.

"School is school," I answered. I wondered how I looked in an apron.

"And this goes on top." Mr. Flandro pressed a paper hat down on top of my damp head.

I nodded, speechless.

He handed me a wet dishcloth. "To begin," he instructed, "keep the tables cleared. The trays are stacked here"—he pointed—"and the trash goes in here. And the mop—"

I must have glanced too often at the hamburgers frying on the grill because he asked, "Are you hungry?"

I acted surprised. "Hungry? Not at all. I was just looking around."

At three o'clock the doors were propped open and the high-school crowd poured in. For the next three hours I was too busy to think about my paper hat or my stomach. At six o'clock I went to the back of the kitchen, put my apron on a shelf, and punched out.

"Same time tomorrow?" I asked, looking at Tom and Mr. Flandro.

"Same time," Tom said. He rubbed his arm across his perspiring forehead.

I glanced around. "Any cold hamburgers?"

Tom nodded toward a pile of wrapped hamburgers. "Help yourself."

I took a couple and put them into a sack. Then two more. Then I shoved in two more. The sack burst, so I took one out and shoved it into my pocket.

I glanced up. Tom and Mr. Flandro were staring at me.

"Uh—," I stammered. "Uh—if it is all right with the management, I know some—ducks."

5

The little critters woke me up, trilling and croaking. I was terrified, thinking the mountains had fallen over on me. I thrashed about, bumping my head, until I realized I was in the backseat of my Jeep.

I sat up fast and looked out the window. The view was limited—green foliage all around, a circle of blue above, and a fierce-looking magpie perched on the hood, pointing a sharp beak at me.

"Caw, caw," he cried.

I reached over the seat and pressed the

36

horn. "Fly, critter."

He flew.

The silence was overwhelming for a few seconds, but then the ruckus began again. Cawing, trilling, croaking.

I rolled up my sleeping bag, wanting to keep a tidy bedroom, then climbed into the front seat for breakfast. I opened the sack of cold hamburgers and felt a renewed sense of confidence in myself. I had provided food. I had provided shelter. Things were not perfect, but they were better than yesterday when I awoke to Baggy Legs. This morning I could enjoy a leisurely breakfast out on the patio.

I opened the driver's door, squeezed through, and sat on the fender. I could see I had a lot more trampling down to do, but I had time for that. I could build shelves. And a garage.

During breakfast I watched a *National Geographic* special: squirrels darting up and down the trees, quail scurrying across the ground, magpies and blue jays flitting from branch to branch, and bugs creeping. All were intent on staying alive. As was I.

At seven o'clock I got ready for school. I jumped on my mountain bike and pedaled down the canyon, wondering how late I was. It's that school bell thing.

I was four days late, I found out, when I went to the office of Mrs. Green, the counselor who was taking care of transfer students. On her door a note in green ink read: TRANSFER STUDENTS WALK IN.

I walked in.

Mrs. Green sat behind her desk doing the transferring. Three students waited in green vinyl chairs. The color coordination made me nervous and I did not want to sit down. So I stood near the door, shifting from foot to foot.

The lives of transfer students are not private, I found out. I heard everything about the three students ahead of me: names, addresses, telephone numbers, former schools, birthdays. All that private information. Mrs. Green asked it, they told it.

When my turn came I started off saying, "Uh." Deception was a new practice for me, and I had a hard time saying my name.

"Address?" Mrs. Green asked next.

"Uh—402 Canyon Road."

She glanced up. "Canyon Road?"

"Uh—uh—my mom and I just moved here. We are staying with relatives until we find a house. The one we are looking at is just down the block—"

"Telephone?"

"Uh—402–4022."

She looked up again. "The same as your house number?"

I gave a quick smile. "Incredible coincidence."

"Do you have a transcript of credits?"

"Uh—in the mail."

"There is a registration fee—"

"Uh—I'll bring a check tomorrow."

"And the book fee?"

A girl from the green chairs spoke up loudly. "By law she has to admit him—"

Mrs. Green frowned. "I cannot assign a locker without the registration fee."

"I'll carry my books."

The girl spoke up again. "It would save time in the long run if she would just assign him a locker—"

Mrs. Green tapped her fingers on her desk. She was getting nervous. "I really don't have enough information here—"

I pulled out my wallet and showed her my driver's license. I smiled broadly. "I'm this person. And I am a good student."

A bell rang.

"She is making us all late for class," the girl said directly behind me.

"All right, all right," Mrs. Green said, handing me the necessary papers. She dismissed me with a wave of her arm and a sigh.

I like counselors. I don't like to make them nervous.

"My turn," the girl said. "Diantha Dragon, 2025 Eastside Drive—"

I do not like loud girls, and I tried not to

look at her. But as I turned to leave she brushed against me. "Liar," she whispered.

Just one glance and she took my breath away. She was wearing black from her neck to her ankles—a black jersey top and black tights—with a red ruffle around her middle. And red high-top shoes. Her hair stuck up in the air, although some of it fell down her neck. She jingled like wind chimes. A girl like her would definitely cause a traffic jam in Winnemucca.

I hurried out into the hall.

My junior class schedule turned out to be just like my sophomore and freshman years. I had planned to take some extras this year like drama and swimming. I had signed up for them in Winnemucca and again in Seattle, but this time it seemed easier to take what Mrs. Green assigned.

My schedule was English, math, health/P.E., lunch, chemistry, history, and study hall. And it was fine with me.

Since I had already missed English and

most of math, I decided to miss all of health/P.E. and officially start my junior year after lunch. I asked a secretary where the post office was and she told me it was about half a mile from school.

I took off on my bike.

I wrote a postcard to Mrs. Crofts. I said I was here in Red Rock, Idaho, and not to worry, my mother would understand everything. And to please forward all my mail to general delivery. I felt a great sense of relief as I pushed the card through the mail slot. I did not want Mrs. Crofts on my conscience.

In the afternoon I went to chemistry and then history, which turned out to be world history. I sat in the back of each classroom, feeling definitely out of alphabetical order. During study hall I found a seat in an isolated corner of the library and stared at my books. I wondered if anyone had ever gotten into *The Guinness Book of World Records* for eating a book.

Finally the two-thirty bell rang. I shoved my

books into my backpack and pedaled to work.

"Greetings on Thursday," Mr. Flandro said.

I said, "Greetings."

Tom nodded from the grill. The other employees were busy working.

I wiped trays and tables again, keeping an eye on the hamburgers sizzling on the grill. And I noticed four blond girls sitting in a booth next to the one I was cleaning. I do like blondes. They were talking quietly, giggling now and then. The one who did most of the talking had her hair piled up on top of her head, held up there with a plastic butterfly clip. The others had short hair lapping against their long thin necks.

They talked about their drama class—the teacher, the plays they were going to produce, the parts they hoped to get. They were swamped with homework and did not know how they could possibly get it all done. When would they ever ride their bikes again? Right now, they decided. They left without a care in the world.

I remembered the feeling. Pete and I used to talk like that at the Red Bandanna after school. Never once did we notice who cleaned the tables.

I had cares now. And not one friend. And I was desperately tired of cleaning tables. Nausea curled in my stomach and crept up into my throat. I thought I might throw up all over the table I had just cleaned.

Desperately tired is how Mom Miller had felt, too. Her exact words were, "I am tired of teaching second grade, Marty. Desperately tired. And I am lonely."

I still could not believe it. She had never complained before about teaching second grade. After school she put her feet up on a little horsehair footstool in the living room and listened to Mozart. She vacuumed. And she went to her literary club with Pete's mom and Miss Addison.

Each Christmas we decorated a spruce tree with strings of popcorn and colored glass balls. We placed it in front of the living room window for all Winnemucca to see, as every-one else in town did.

We went to church. In fact, Mom Miller had the reputation for being the best pie maker in our church. At a fund-raiser, one of her rhubarb pies sold for a hundred dollars. The secret, she told me, was freezing the pie crust ingredients first.

And lonely with me in the house? I would never forgive Mr. Joe Wonderful.

At six o'clock Mr. Flandro walked over to me. He looked desperately tired, too. "Tom mentioned we pay every other Saturday," he said. "It keeps employees showing up on Saturdays."

"I'll be here," I said quickly.

"What I want to know," he continued, "is if you want a small check this Saturday for a partial week, or if you want me to add it to the next check?"

"Uh—" I tried to sound casually indifferent. I shrugged. "What the heck. I'll take a small check."

I stuffed cold hamburgers into a sack. What the heck? If he did not give me a check on Saturday, I would not be around to collect the next one.

"I'll be in Saturday, for sure," I said. "What time do you hand out the checks? I can come in anytime. What time?"

"It will be ready when you leave at six," he said. "Here on the shelf." He hesitated. "Do you need an advance, Marty? For any reason?"

"Am I taking too many?" I started pulling hamburgers out of the sack. I was not good at desperation since I had never practiced it, either. I did not like the feeling. Nor did I like Mr. Flandro's questions.

"Of course not," he said. "They would just go into the bin outside. I hate to think of it with all the hungry people in the world, but—"

"Well, thanks"—I shoved in a few more hamburgers—"I need to hurry home. I am swamped with homework. See you tomorrow. Same time?"

"Same time," he answered.

I headed for the canyon, but after a few blocks I stopped under a tree on someone's lawn and began eating the hamburgers, one after the other. I tried to eat slowly, chewing each bite thirty times before swallowing. I had read about starving people who died after eating a solid meal again. I was not about to die eating.

I burped all the way up the canyon.

My camp was so well hidden I missed it myself and had to backtrack before I found it. The phony gate worked. My Jeep was still there, splattered with magpie droppings. I squeezed inside and crawled into the back to relax. It felt good to be in my own home again.

I awoke suddenly. It was dark and quiet. Outside, two large bright eyes blinked in the foliage. I opened the door cautiously and stretched my legs. The bright eyes disappeared.

I didn't know what time of day it was or,

for that matter, what day. It could be Saturday night—and I had slept through work. I realized I would need to follow a better schedule and eat, sleep, and work at regular times. I could not miss work if I wanted to eat. And I wanted to eat.

Back inside I switched on the overhead light and checked my watch. I had only slept four hours. I opened my history book and read a few pages. But I could not concentrate on daily life in Mesopotamia. I was worrying about the overhead light killing the battery.

I ate another hamburger and then made a list of necessities to take care of on Saturday, right on the inside cover of my history book with a ballpoint pen, invalidating any future book refund.

The list:

> Food
> Flashlight
> Laundromat
> NATIONAL GEOGRAPHIC
> Haircut

Gas
Post office box
Book fee

I read it over, debating the order of the items. Then, still worried about the battery, I turned off the light and climbed back into the bedroom.

For some reason, the memory of all those pies I had eaten over the years flashed through my mind: fresh peach, mile-high strawberry, rhubarb, banana cream, and lemon meringue. Five hundred pies, easily. And still I was a skinny runt, expecting each month to extend to six feet.

This could be the month, the very night, in fact, and I was confined to the width of a CJ7 Jeep. What luck!

I reached over and rapped on the window. "Good night, little critters," I called. And curled up in my sleeping bag.

Dutch apple, pumpkin chiffon, chocolate cream, key lime. And magpie?

6

Saturday at dawn, I christened my place the Camp of Many Critters. I rolled down the window and shouted, "Hark!" For a moment there was silence. Then I called out my Camp Oath, just like a teenager of ancient Athens, according to Mr. Williams in fifth period.

> *I will never bring disgrace on this my*
> *Camp of Many Critters.*
> *I will not litter.*
> *I will not trample foliage unnecessarily.*
> *I will show respect to all critters flying,*

50

creeping, or just looking.
I will step softly on the ones too
minuscule to be seen.
Thus in all these ways I will transmit
this camp, not only not less, but
greater and more beautiful than it was
transmitted to me.

The critters responded with a horrendous clatter, which I took for applause.

Since it was too noisy to go back to sleep, I shook out my sleeping bag and rolled it up on the backseat. So my bed was made. Then I sorted through my clothes and stacked the dirty ones on the front seat. I needed a laundromat immediately.

I rolled the dirty clothes into a ball and pressed through the trees toward the creek I could hear in the distance. And I will swear on my world history book that daily life in Mesopotamia four thousand years ago was no more primitive than this. When I finally reached the stream I collapsed, tattered and bleeding, on top of my dirty laundry.

As the cold, clear water turned murky, I wondered if I had just polluted the water supply of Woodland High. I wondered if this same murky water would spray out of the shower over my head in the locker room on Monday morning. I wondered how much *National Geographic* paid topless women to smile as they scrubbed clothing on the banks of the Euphrates. I also wondered if lack of food was affecting my mind, or if it had worked this way before.

Going back was worse. The scrub oak showed no sign that I had ever passed that way, and the wet laundry was twice as heavy as the dry. When at last I reached the Camp of Many Critters, I felt as if I had returned home, an old man, from a long voyage.

I hung my wet socks over the open window of the driver's door and the other things I spread over the hood. By that time I was ready for breakfast. I ate three cold hamburgers on the patio.

After, in the Jeep, I worked on my shopping list, starting with peanut butter. I had read in you-know-where that the average American boy eats 1,500 peanut butter sandwiches before high school graduation. I would reach that goal, easily.

I did not know how Mom Miller organized her shopping list, alphabetically or by basic food groups. I had never cared enough to ask. But I wrote my list by Desire: peanut butter, milk, bagels, peanut butter, milk, bagels.

I clutched my forehead and groaned in despair. Was I fooling myself that I could survive in this primitive camp? Regardless of my lofty Camp Oath, I could be facing starvation, hypothermia, asphyxiation, accident, fire, kidnapping. Or prosecution.

A large magpie flew down from an overhanging branch and hopped around on my wet underwear. He hopped right up to the windshield and stared at me.

"What do you want, Maggie?" I asked. He had been here before.

He pecked at the windshield.

"What, Maggie?"

When I knew what he wanted it was too late. A big white blob splashed down on my underwear. Then he lifted his wings and flew off. "Caw, caw." I should have known he did not care.

I thought about school. My two days at Woodland High had been miserable. In English, first period, I recognized one of the blond girls from the Burger Box. She sat a few seats up from me and across the aisle. I smiled, but she did not notice me.

In history Mr. Williams checked the roll silently with a seating chart, until he came to the new students in the back.

"Martin J. Miller," he bellowed.

"Here," I said. He did not look happy to see me.

"Diantha Dragon," he bellowed. It was the girl in black who jingled. She did not answer.

Mr. Williams repeated her name, glaring over his glasses.

"Do you want a picture ID?" she asked. She said that for my benefit and I did not look at her.

Everyone else turned around to look. She stared them all down. I guess I was looking because she winked at me.

I turned my head fast and planned not to look again. I do not like black jerseys and jewelry. But my eyes just kept wandering back.

I had attended school for two days and I remembered only the faces of two girls. I wondered if I could be girl crazy.

I drove my Jeep to work and arrived early. I had allowed time to look for a grocery store, so I would not waste time after work. As soon as I was down the canyon I saw a grocery store on every corner. Some, however, could have been grocery store mirages.

At the Burger Box I looked for my paycheck on the shelf. I felt on top of my apron and under it and along the entire shelf.

Mr. Flandro noticed. "Your check will be there at six, Marty."

I wished I had not looked so hard.

The store was busy, but it was a different crowd—families with young children. One family was singing "Happy Birthday" to a little girl with ketchup on her face. While they sang, the mother stuck a flickering pink candle in the top of each hamburger bun.

Mr. Flandro beamed. "A birthday every Saturday," he said. "And ketchup on the seats."

Ketchup all over the seats was more like it. After a while Mr. Flandro gave me a promotion. He told me to be a trainee at the counter under a boy named Bert.

After training for five minutes I knew what to do, but Bert told me not to talk to anyone, just to observe. I stood at his elbow like a dummy for the rest of the day. Customers tried to order from me and tried to pay me, but I stood mute, nodding my head toward Bert.

At six o'clock I was out of there, my paycheck clutched in my hand.

I stopped at the first grocery store I saw, in case the others were mirages. It was a little store on a corner called Mike's Grocery. I filled a basket with food and a flashlight.

At the checkout counter I hovered over my

mound of goods. "Careful," I said as the girl tossed the bananas onto the scale. I did not have money to waste on bruised bananas. And I bagged the groceries myself.

Although I had planned to wait until I reached camp to eat, the aroma from the bag overwhelmed me. I ate in Mike's Parking Lot. Along with the regular cold hamburger, I had a banana, a half quart of milk, and a bagel dipped in chunky peanut butter.

Back in camp I ate the same things again, in the same order. For the first time in a week, I felt good. I felt so good I honked the horn. Then I honked it again—long and loud. I laughed and sang and ate a chocolate bar for the finale. And honked the horn again.

When I heard the sirens I realized how foolish I had been. In my complete self-satisfaction I had let down my guard and had given away my hiding place. And someone had reported honking in the trees.

The sirens screamed up the canyon road, closer and closer. I thought I might run down

57

to the stream and hide, but I knew I could not survive without my Jeep.

I jumped out, shoved my laundry and the groceries into the scrub oak, and hid my bike behind a pine tree. Then I made a pretense of collecting leaves—

The sirens were deafening. The leaves trembled in my hands. Of course I had read the sign NO OVERNIGHT CAMPING. And of course, I understood the consequences. The sirens passed and moved on up the road, becoming fainter.

I leaned against the Jeep, waiting. I waited for a long time, expecting the sirens to return. Cars passed, but none stopped.

I crept out to the road to check the phony gate and the Jeep tracks. The camouflage was still good. I felt better, and I hurried back to the car. I put batteries in my new flashlight and ate another bagel with peanut butter. Heck, I could survive anything: starvation, hypothermia, asphyxiation, prosecution—

I leaned back in the seat and unabashedly rubbed my stomach, a revolting habit my uncle John displayed at Thanksgiving dinner.

He only did it once that I saw, but then he and Aunt Hildy came to Thanksgiving dinner at our house only once. Aunt Hildy and Uncle John flew all the way from Niceville, Florida, to spend Thanksgiving with us. Aunt Hildy was anxious to see how her brother's son was turning out.

Mom Miller and I expected people from a town called Niceville to be nicer than other people. But it was a false assumption. They gossiped about relatives. They complained about taxes and Aunt Hildy's gallbladder operation. They criticized the Pope. Uncle John belched out loud. And he pulled up his shirt and rubbed his stomach.

I have thought about him every Thanksgiving since, and that night in camp. I also thought about the large magpie who visited me. I was beginning to like the wild little critter.

Things were looking up: a Camp of Many Critters, a red Jeep, a flashlight, and a bagel with chunky peanut butter.

7

I made a list on the inside back cover of my
history book of additional necessities:

> Earmuffs
> Ice cubes
> Reading lamp
> Microwave oven
> Automatic washer
> Calendar
> Toothpaste
> Cell phone
> Trust fund

I read a lot of world history by flashlight. The little critters did not like the light, however, and also my arm became tired. So after work I started driving to the public library on Foothill Road to study.

The first night—with no moon in the sky—I passed my camp and did not find it until after midnight. The critters made a loud protest.

I spent a lot of time sitting in the dark, thinking. I thought about my list and wondered how long it would take me to buy all those things. I thought about the poor people of the world and the rich people. Then I narrowed it down to the poor and rich of the United States.

I decided if everyone in the United States would send me one dollar, it would not hurt anyone. And it would certainly help me. I thought that before it was too late I should place an ad in the newspaper:

**To all U.S. Citizens
Send $1 Only to
Martin J. Miller
c/o This Newspaper
Soon!**

Well, it was a thought. Instead, I emptied a shoe
box I found among my things, printed a message on the side, and stuck it over the antenna:

M.J.M. Fund
Give!

The next morning I parked my Jeep in front
of the school where it could be seen easily.
During third period I looked down from the
second-floor window and saw that it was
still there.

After school I wanted to rush out to my
car, but I was a coward. I went out the back
door and ran to work. When I returned, my
Jeep was alone in the parking lot. At
Woodland High no one much cared about me
or my old red Jeep.

I pulled the shoe box off the antenna and drove fast toward the canyon. But when I reached Mike's Grocery, I pulled into his parking lot to count the contributions:

> 6 pennies
> 1 note with message: Life happens!
> 3 obscene phrases
> 2 wads of gum

I may have learned one of life's important lessons in that parking lot, but its meaning was unclear to me.

To save gas, I stayed in camp and read history by flashlight, despite the ruckus. I began thinking about all the cities of the world, ancient and modern. And I realized that the only city I would ever love is Winnemucca, Nevada, where I was born and where I intend to die and be buried next to my dad in the grassless cemetery just off Main Street. No matter where I found myself in the cities of the world—New York City, Istanbul, Athens, Seattle, or Red Rock—I would always be just ten miles from Winnemucca in my heart.

A wind came up at dusk, tossing the aspen trees and bending the tops of the pines. All night it screeched and howled. Twigs and branches snapped off the trees and dropped on the hardtop. I sank deep into my sleeping bag, wondering if this could possibly be the end of the world.

In the morning the Camp of Many Critters was covered with a mantle of golden leaves. The critters were hushed. I tiptoed around, trying not to disturb one golden leaf. It seemed as if all the cities of the world had blown away and the world was new. And I was Adam.

Old Walt knew how it felt:

> *As Adam, early in the morning,*
> *Walking forth from the bower, refresh'd*
> *with sleep;*
> *Behold me where I pass—*

I carried my bike out to the road and took off down the canyon. Looking for my Eve.

• • •

"How do you like the locker I got for you?"
Diantha Dragon shimmered in front of the
locker next to mine.

"Well, D-D-" I choked on the name.

"Dani Dragon," she said. "You'll get used to
it." She turned the combination of a hot pink
padlock. "So where do you want to go?"

"Go?" I closed my locker and stared at her.
She had red sequins on her tennis shoes.
"Uh—I'm going to class." I took off.

I dashed to first period and slumped down
in my seat. Blond Lisa turned at her desk and
smiled in my direction. So I sat up and said,
"How do you like Red Rock?"

"Who?"

"Red Rock," I mumbled.

"It's where I live." She wrinkled her nose.

"I know." I would be stammering soon.

"How do you like it?"

"I like it fine," I said.

She stared at me for a moment, laughed,
and turned back to her desk.

That was all the talking to girls I did that day.

8

THURSDAY, SEPTEMBER 13

At noon I rode my bike to the post office.

I calculated that if someone in Paris dropped a letter into a corner mailbox and a carrier picked it up that afternoon and took it to the main post office, it should reach Seattle in one week. Then Mrs. Crofts would forward it to Red Rock—

A general delivery letter was waiting from Mrs. Crofts. She told me to go to a pay phone and call her and answer a few questions immediately. So I did.

"Yes, I am intact."

. . .

"It is just an adjective."

. . .

"Yes, Burgess did throw my things out the window."

. . .

"No, he did not throw me."

. . .

"Yes, I am staying with relatives, my uncle John and aunt Hildy."

. . .

"No, I do not know why their phone number is unlisted. That is just the way they like it."

. . .

"No, I am not calling for money."

Then Mrs. Crofts raised her voice. "What will I tell your mother when she calls?"

Things I tell my mother, Mrs. Crofts does not need to know. But until then—

"Tell her I am intact."

. . .

"It is just an adjective."

. . .

"Tell her Burgess did throw my things out the window."

. . .

"No, he did not throw me—"

Mrs. Crofts groaned. I knew she cared.

After I hung up, I walked back inside the post office. "Any other letters?" I asked.

"Sorry." The clerk shook her head.

"Have you checked in the cracks—places where letters and cards slip through?" I leaned over the countertop.

The clerk stiffened. "We don't have any places like that."

"But, just the same, it happens," I said. "Just last week I read in the paper about a woman in Butte, Montana, who received a postcard from her father forty years after he died. The postcard was found in a crack behind a cupboard during refurbishment of the post office. The woman was seventy-three years old."

"Really?" The clerk tapped her fingers on

the counter and glanced around. I was the only customer there.

"Would you like me to bring the article?" I asked.

"Not really." She tapped faster. "Have you thought of renting a P.O. box?"

I like postal clerks. I do not like to make them nervous. "I am saving for one," I said. "See you tomorrow."

The next day the clerk handed me three letters, all of which had arrived just that morning, she said. For two weeks I had been waiting for a letter, and then three came on the same day—a postcard from Kennedy Airport and two letters from Paris.

Mom Miller wanted to know how I was and how I liked school and if I had enough spending money. She explained that Mrs. Crofts would see that all my needs were taken care of, which she had also explained before.

The rest was travelogue. I could have read it myself in *National Geographic* had I wanted to know about it.

She and Mr. Joe had been up the Eiffel Tower and to Notre Dame Cathedral. They had visited the Louvre, where they entered by way of the new I. M. Pei pyramid. This new structure in front of the old museum was jarring to the senses, Mr. Joe felt. She liked it fine. Mr. Joe's feet ached, but they both felt it was worth the discomfort to stand a few minutes of a lifetime before the Mona Lisa.

The following day they were planning to go out to Versailles, if Mr. Joe's feet held up.

The second letter described the glories of Versailles, so apparently his feet held up.

Just *National Geographic* stuff. Nothing personal. Except Mr. Joe's swollen feet, which I did not count. Of course, at the end of each letter Mom Miller said that she missed me terribly. But it was canceled out by the next sentence—she was having a marvelous time.

I shoved the letters into my backpack, wishing they had never arrived after all. They had only provoked the same old questions.

And that old nausea.

She had not married him for money, surely. We had a teacher's salary and retirement for the future. Maybe she was worried about getting old and having a gallbladder operation like Aunt Hildy had. Now that I thought about it, I did remember seeing her lying around occasionally with a heating pad on her side. Could she have married him because of her gallbladder?

I pedaled back to school to Mr. Fields's chemistry.

I had never written a letter to my mother. I know that may sound unbelievable to boys who have gone to summer camp and to their grandparents' farm. I never went to those places. We went to the beach in California and to the mountains in Utah. But we both went, and so we did not need to write letters.

Pete always wanted to be an only child like me, although not because of letter writing. At his house things were always getting broken.

I always wanted a dad like Pete's—someone big to wrestle with on the living-room floor. Mom Miller said she was keeping an eye out for one. When she brought home Mr. Joe Wonderful she thought she had really found a good one. She was smiling all over.

After one look I told her thanks, but no thanks. He was not a wrestler. Besides, I was sixteen and did not need one anymore.

She cried in her bedroom after he left that night, because of what I said. I felt like crying, but I sat like a stone on my bed, listening to her through the wall.

In study hall I tried to write a letter. But after moving my pencil around my notebook for almost an hour, I found out it is impossible to write a letter to your mother with your peers in the same room.

Back in camp I pulled Mom Miller's letters out of my backpack and read them again by flashlight. With a ballpoint pen I crossed out all mention of Mr. Joe Wonderful.

I wrote a short letter:

Dear Mom Miller,
I am intact.
How is your gallbladder?
Your son,
Martin J. Miller

I sat in the dark, contemplating my place in the universe, trying to come up with a formula. Maybe I was a chemistry experiment, just existing in Red Rock, Idaho.

But I had existed for two weeks and, therefore, I could exist for two more. And two more.

I rolled down the window and beamed the flashlight around camp. "I don't need anybody," I called out. "Nobody at all."

9

On a Saturday in September the critters tried to warn me about the deer hunt, setting up a horrendous ruckus. But, human as I am, I ignored them.

I rolled up my dirty laundry and forayed down to the Euphrates. The scrub oak was turning red, the quaking aspen yellow. The air quivered with the scent of musk and pine. When I stepped out of the trees, I was feeling about as good as Martin J. Miller can feel.

Then shots rang out. I dropped to the ground and covered my head with my laundry, shivering with fear. I wondered who would want to shoot me—besides Burgess, Mrs. Crofts, and the postal clerk.

I waited a few minutes, then crawled on my stomach back to the trees. I was bruised, but still intact. Back at camp, I dug out a red flannel shirt that was stashed in the back of my Jeep, and I planned to wear it until deer season was over. I do not like flying bullets.

"How do you like the locker I got for you?" It was that Dragon girl again, turning her hot pink padlock.

She came in by way of the back door, each day wearing a different ruffle over her black tights. She paraded around the halls, showing off, until the first bell rang. Then she dashed over to the lockers all breathless and ruffly and attacked me. "How do you like the locker I got for you?"

So this day in my red shirt I said, "I like it fine."

And she said, "So where do you want to go?"

"Go?" She was ruffly and noisy.

"After school."

"Uh—I work until six."

"After six then. Where?" She should be in a school play.

"Uh—uh"—I was beginning to stammer again—"I need to go to a laundromat."

"Where do you work?"

"At the Burger Box."

"See you at six." In a flash she was gone.

I was stunned. Pete and I did not date girls, not girls who picked us up, anyway. We went to movies with girls, but we did the asking and we bought the popcorn. And the girls wore jeans.

I shrugged and walked to class. I did not expect Dani Dragon to show up.

It snows early in Red Rock, as early as October because everyone in town prays for it, according to Phillip Harkness who sat next to me in chemistry. He lives to ski.

I live to eat. And I was thinking about it

during Mr. Fields's lecture on photosynthesis. Something must have shown on my face because he paused and looked straight at me. "What is on your mind, Miller?" he asked.

So I told him. "Food."

"Food, you say?"

"Why can't we humans use photosynthesis to get our energy the same as plants?" I asked. "We could recharge each morning. Eating is so inefficient. It takes too much time and too much money."

Mr. Fields stared. The class stared.

"It was just a thought," I murmured.

"Any other suggestions, Miller?" Mr. Fields was not sarcastic, just tired of hearing his own voice.

"There is something," I added. "I think it should rain and snow on schedule. Perhaps every seventh day or the last week of the month. Think of all the picnics in the canyons—" I paused and took a deep breath. "Well, that is just something else that I think."

Mr. Fields looked around at the twittering

class. "At least someone is thinking," he said.

Then the bell rang.

"Say, Miller"—Phillip moved over to me—"about this photosynthesis. What happens when you go to the beach? You know, you sit down to read a book, you doze off, you wake up. And you are two hundred pounds heavier!"

"It was just a thought," I said.

"Well, pray for snow," he said, "and we'll go skiing." He glided down the hall, practicing his form.

For a few minutes there, I thought I was normal again and I began getting that old Moosehood feeling. I would go skiing with Phillip Harkness. I would go to his house after school with half a dozen cold hamburgers. We would kick around and then wax our skis in his basement.

Then one day he would ask, "Hey, Miller, where do you live?"

I would have to say that I was breaking the law living in a canyon with no overnight living allowed. I was always on the lookout for the sheriff. For mad hunters. And for large bright eyes in the bushes.

I looked down the hall at all the normal teenagers and I hated Mr. Joe for doing this to me. I could not be friends with Phillip Harkness. To survive, I had to stay friendless.

Diantha Dragon showed up, honking an old green Chevrolet that must have been her mother's. She rolled down the window and yelled, "Over here, Marty." Anyone could hear her.

I looked around self-consciously.

"Over here, Marty," she called again. "Come and get in this ugly old car." She revved the engine and pulled up so close she could have run over my leg.

I grabbed my roll of dirty laundry from the Jeep and tucked it under my arm. "Where did you get the Chevy?" I opened the door and settled in the passenger's seat.

"This ugly car belongs to my mother," she

said. "After dark it can pass for a black Mercedes. And when it snows—"

"It's a nice car for a mother," I said. I offered her a cold hamburger, which she accepted. I ate three.

Dragon drove downtown and pulled up in front of the Klean Machine Laundromat. "Do you ski?" she asked.

"Uh—I did once," I said.

"What happened?"

"I got down the hill," I said. "That happened. Isn't that what is supposed to happen?" I do not tell total strangers that I never had a father to take me skiing and that Mom Miller braved the winter road to Lake Tahoe only once.

Dragon turned off the ignition and dropped the keys into a large canvas bag with a cat's picture on the front. "Now ask me if I ski," she said. "Then we can call it a conversation."

"Do you ski?"

"No." She opened the car door, pulling the

canvas bag after her. "I'm new to Red Rock, too. Remember?"

I bounded up the steps to the laundromat and held the door open. "Where did you move from?" I asked.

"Somewhere in Missouri," she said.

I did not ask any more questions.

The laundromat was warm and steamy and appeared safe from hunters' bullets. Several other people were there, lounging on the worn vinyl benches, watching their clothes whirl around.

I walked to the far end and selected the last machine on the row. I took off my red shirt, wrapped it around my dirty laundry, and shoved it into the washer.

Dragon sat on a bench and watched other people watching their clothes. She seemed very interested in other people's underclothes. After a while she came down and sat in front of my washer.

"Your underwear is pink," she said. "Pink underwear, pink socks, pink towels."

I stared, and when the washer stopped I took out my red and pink clothing. I wanted to cry.

"Leo 'Socks' Burnette," I said.

"Who's Leo?"

"A kid I knew in Winnemucca," I said. "Somewhere in Nevada. He wore pink socks and pink underwear from kindergarten right up to high school. Kids used to tease him. 'Leo, where did you get those pink socks?' Leo just shrugged. He didn't know."

"Don't cry," Dragon said. She grabbed my clothes and shoved them in a dryer and pushed in the coins. Then she went back to underwear watching.

Right there in the Klean Machine Laundromat I choked up over Leo Burnette. I thought of him always late for school because he was rummaging through drawers, searching for the white socks he had received for Christmas. Never finding them because his mother had received red towels.

I wanted to go to a pay phone and call Leo

and tell him he could be in the Moose Club with me and Pete. I felt really down-and-out.

The dryer stopped and I put on my faded red shirt and rolled my other things into a ball. Dragon was waiting at the door. Her cat bag was bulging.

"What do you have in there?" I asked. "A cat?"

In the Burger Box parking lot she emptied the bag: socks, underwear, towels, T-shirts. All white.

"What the heck—" I said.

"For you." She jingled.

"Uh—I do not like other people's socks," I said. "I have enough trouble with my own."

"Remember Leo Burnette."

"Thanks anyway, D-Dragon," I stammered.

She shoved the stuff into my arms and gave me a push out the door. So I carried it all over to my Jeep, dumped it in the back, and drove up the canyon.

The little critters were glad to see me and I was glad to be back in camp. Maggie flew down and hopped around on the hood, showing off for me. I told him all about my date with a glittering thief.

After a while they all calmed down. The camp shimmered golden in the moonlight. I thought about Leo Burnette again. And Pete. And Phillip Harkness. Then I began thinking about all the people in the world—the ones who are happy and the ones who are hurting, the bullies and their victims, the loudmouths and the shy ones. The just regulars, as I used to be.

But I was no longer just regular. Not with flying bullets and other people's socks. Cold hamburgers. And no one to talk to except a wild magpie. I thought I might as well go back to Seattle and see what stringy-haired Burgess was up to.

Someone else would have to pray for snow for Phillip Harkness.

10

The next morning a flock of redbirds woke me with an amazing chorus. I vaulted from my sleeping bag, over the front seat, and out the door.

Redbirds were in the trees, in the bushes, on the grass, and on top of my Jeep, singing like crazy. Suddenly they took flight in a whirl of red and disappeared over the tall pines.

I stood transfixed, watching the empty sky. It was a good omen. My camp was safe, safer than the house on Ivy Cliff Drive with Burgess.

After a while I pulled on my clothes and headed down the canyon to school.

Also, there was this girl in red high-top shoes—

Dragon had taped an oversized message on my locker: *Meet me at six, Marty. You know where*.

Anyone could read it.

And at six o'clock she pulled up in her old green car at the Burger Box. She honked the horn and stuck her head out the window. "Let's go shoplifting," she called.

Anyone could hear.

"What's in the sack?" she called.

I relaxed my grip. "Burgers."

"We'll eat in the car then."

We ate cold hamburgers driving around the town—up on the old avenues, around the cemetery, and south to the mall.

"Don't you ever run out of gas?" I asked.

"I never run out of gas," she said. She pulled up at the Southtown Mall.

"I don't have much cash tonight," I mumbled. I did not have any cash, but when I did there was a long list inside the cover of my history book—

"Who does?" She stepped out of the car swinging her cat bag.

I followed.

The mall at night was quiet and the clerks tired and indifferent. We walked through the shops, looking, wondering who would buy all those things.

"Wait here," Dragon said, and she disappeared inside a corner restaurant.

I shuffled around a few minutes. Then I remembered Dragon had her cat bag, and I rushed to the restaurant window and pressed my face into some stranger's face.

Then Dragon came out. Her hair was sticking straight up in the air, held up by half a dozen helium balloons.

I stared.

"It's the real me," she said.

We walked over to a fountain and sat down

on a low wall in front. Anyone could see.

"We have a lot in common, Marty," she said.

I just kept staring at her hair.

"We are both new to Red Rock and we need to stick together. It makes it easier. You know—counselors, teachers, kids at school."

I opened my mouth—

"You would not have a locker without my help, Marty. Imagine telling Mrs. Green that made-up story. I've been new before—"

"I—I don't need anybody," I stammered.

"Yes, you do." She was a sassy girl.

Later, in the car, she turned on the overhead light and turned the radio up loud. Freebies tumbled out of her cat bag: crayons, vitamin pills, bookmarks, perfume samples, apples, crackers, and peppermints.

"You are having fun, aren't you, Marty?" she shouted above the music. "Not the whole world on your shoulders?"

Riding around all night, balloons bouncing in my face. Maybe I was having fun. But I didn't think so. There were things sitting on my shoulders. I could make a long list.

Still, when she asked, "Tomorrow night, then?" I said, "Sure, why not?"

On Saturday we drove down to the old part of town to the antiques shops. They have weird names. The one we went in was called Older Than You. We parked in the rear and ran around to the front, pushing against a whining wind. A painted wooden Indian stood guard at the door. He looked cold.

The shop was like a museum inside with paintings in ornate wooden frames, old-fashioned mirrors, gramophones, and canopied beds. And high on one wall a shaggy buffalo head stared down at us.

One room was stacked with old books, yellowed and dusty. Another displayed household items of indeterminate use. Also toys and knickknacks from long before our time. Little signs here and there read: IF YOUR HEART LOVES IT, BUY IT.

I picked up a little wooden duck with the paint peeling off its feathers. It reminded me of the ducks in Homeless Park where I had slept that first night in Red Rock when I had fled from Burgess—tough old Burgess, who probably wasn't tough at all by himself. But I was far away from him now.

Dragon sidled up to me. She had a fringed lampshade over her head. So I picked up a wooden cane leaning against a table and staggered around with it.

We paraded through all the rooms—Dragon waltzing with the lampshade on her head and I limping along with the old cane. In the mirrors we could see the clerk following behind, scowling.

After a while we went back out to the parking lot, laughing. In the car Dragon pulled out the little wooden duck from her cat bag.

"For you," she whispered, pressing it into my hands. "The wooden Indian was bolted down."

I wanted to throw the stolen thing out the

window into the wind and never see it again. But I also wanted the laughter to last. I was beginning to like ruffles and glitter. Heck, I was beginning to like them a lot.

I shoved the duck in my pocket and put my arms around Dragon. I shut my eyes and kissed her—on her ear. But it was close.

"You are some kisser, Marty," she said.

"Do you want to go to a movie?" Dragon asked on Monday after work.

"Not tonight," I said. She was using every minute of my life.

But we went. Every night that week we went to a movie. Since Red Rock has only two theaters, we saw only two movies. But we saw them over and over again—a comedy about two old crooks and a World War II film that scared us more each time we went.

After the movies we talked.

"Do you miss Missouri?" I asked.

"I don't even miss Nebraska."

"Nebraska?"

"That's where I lived before Missouri. Now I'm from Idaho. I'm at home anywhere. Not like you and that Winnemucca town."

Then she asked, "So why did you leave?"

I did not want to talk about it. So I mumbled. "The reason was Mr. Joe Wonderful from Seattle, and he wanted us to move up there where green grass grows."

She laughed. "And—what happened up there?"

"Burgess."

"There's always a Burgess." She laughed again and I decided not to talk any more about him.

At the end of the week, after all those movies, she said, "Let's go to your house."

"M-my house?" I began to stammer.

"Sure. The one at 402 Canyon Road. The one with the same phone number: 402-402-402—"

I ignored her remark. "What about your house?" I asked. She had turned off the car engine and it was getting cold.

"I don't even go to my house," she said. "I just sleep there."

"Why is that?" I asked.

"I don't like the old geezer my mom lives with."

"What does the old geezer do?"

"Nothing." She shrugged.

"Nothing?"

"Nothing." She tossed her head and her mismatched earrings—a crescent moon and a howling coyote—shimmered in a flash of moonlight.

"He must do something," I said.

"He buttons his shirts up to the very top button," she said. "That's what he does. He looks as if he is going to choke to death all the time."

I thought of my new stepfather.

"By any chance," I asked, "does he collect coffee tables?"

"He is too stingy to collect anything," she said. "That's the reason he uses every button. He paid for those buttons and he is going to use them or else—"

"Why did your mom marry him?" I asked.

She shrugged. "Who has reasons for anything?"

"I do," I mumbled. "Mom Miller and I do."

"What I like to do," Dragon said, "is break rules. Like my ten o'clock curfew on school nights. That's why I stay out until midnight. It makes them furious."

"I see," I said. But I did not see at all. "At our house we follow rules."

"Of course," Dragon said. "And where is Mom Miller now?"

"In Paris—for a time," I said. "On vacation."

Dragon smiled. "After sixteen years of you, Marty, I'm sure she needed one."

I bristled and reached for the door handle. What was I doing hanging out with a girl like Diantha Dragon, anyway? She did not appear on any of my lists.

"Where are you going?" She pulled at my jacket sleeve.

"I need to study," I said. "I am failing

chemistry. And English and history and—"

"Let's fail them together at your house," she said. Sitting there in the cold car in the moonlight, wearing those mismatched earrings, she looked like a homeless angel. I felt true Moosehood swell within my chest.

"Okay," I said, "to my place. Follow my Jeep."

But maybe it wasn't true Moosehood that I felt. Maybe what I really felt was lonely.

"It needs Chinese lanterns" was what she said.

I stood in the center of camp shaking my head.

"They could light up the whole place," she said, "starting in this tree." She ran to the large pine in front of the Jeep.

"Stop!" I shouted and waved my arms. "The little critters won't like it."

"Sor-ry," she said, not acting the least bit sorry. "We could start them over here." She pretended to carry lanterns and drape them around the trees and bushes. "We could have a party!"

"Not so loud," I whispered. "And no parties."

"You are as nervous as an old bat," she said. "Relax. This is a great place. How did you ever find it?"

I began pacing up and down, thinking of the NO CAMPING sign at the mouth of the canyon. "Let's go," I said. "I should not have brought you here. It must be kept a secret, you realize, or I will end up in Mrs. Green's office. Or in jail. Promise you won't tell anyone, Dragon. Promise?"

She laughed. "It's too good not to tell."

"Just don't tell, Dragon. Just don't." I was feeling as nervous as that old bat she knew about.

"Come on," I said, taking her arm. "Let's go."

She looked surprised. "I thought we were going to study," she said.

"You are too noisy."

She pulled away from me. "With hunters

shooting up and down this canyon, I am too noisy?"

"There are dozens of little critters around us that we cannot see," I whispered, "and they do not like to be disturbed. Skunks and porcupines. And Maggie." I waved my arms about. "And big ones, too. Cougars and bobcats."

"Oh-h," she squealed.

"And besides," I stammered, "I—I have a Camp Oath."

"A Camp Oath?" She slapped her right hand over her heart.

I leaned against the Jeep. "Pete and I decided we are going to do it right."

"Who's Pete? Who's Maggie? Do what right?"

"You know. Life."

"You mean the Ten Commandments?"

"It's a good list," I said. I did not mention my other ones.

"Wow," she whispered. She was standing on the tiptoes of her red high-tops, about to topple over. "So if I join, no more shoplifting?

And home by ten on weeknights?"

"You don't join—" I shoved my hands into my jacket pockets. Why was I telling her all this? I didn't even know what I was talking about. But there she stood on tiptoes, whispering and smiling at me.

"Come on," I said, reaching out. "Time to go."

"But," she whispered, "I need to study world history—" She toppled over and I caught her.

"That is what I was saying," I whispered back. "Time to go study. By flashlight."

Later when I was alone I paced back and forth over the crackling leaves. Mostly we had studied world history. And I had done a little better at kissing. But I had given away the key to my camp. Handed it over to a girl who glittered.

I had been safe in Little Red Rock Canyon, except for a few flying bullets. But now what, old Walt? Now what?

11

I don't know when I started craving lasagna. It was some cold night in October. I was missing Mom Miller. And Pete. Leo "Socks" Burnette. And all those other people in Winnemucca. I had been avoiding Dragon. I needed to keep a low profile in the canyon, and she was too noisy.

Yet as I sat alone in the darkness, I thought perhaps a paper lantern here and there might not be such a bad idea. I thought how Pete would like to be camping out with me. And then I began thinking how much

99

Pete and I like lasagna.

After a while the craving became so intense that I took money from my savings envelope and drove down the canyon to an all-night market. Only two squares of lasagna were left in the deli counter.

"Any discount after midnight?" I asked.

The woman shook her head, but she threw in a free plastic fork.

It was raining when I left the store, and before I reached the canyon the rain had turned to snow. I had prayed for snow for Phillip Harkness, not realizing I would have to drive in it. My Jeep skidded across the road a couple of times, but fortunately no one else was out in the middle of the night. Going up the canyon I honked at every curve in the road. I was worried about sliding off the road and disappearing down a deep gully and never being able to eat the lasagna.

Back in camp, I held a lasagna festival. I turned on the radio, the overhead light, and the heater. I ignored the battery. I pulled on a couple of sweaters and tied one around my head. The lasagna was cold, but I was warm.

And I remembered Winnemucca.

Once when I was too young to know the consequences, I told Mom Miller that I would like lasagna for my birthday since it was my favorite food.

"Since when?" She looked surprised.

"Since yesterday," I told her. I had eaten it over at Pete's house.

Every year since she has made lasagna for my birthday. She makes it completely from scratch, including the wide noodles which she hangs over the kitchen chairs according to instructions in an old Italian cookbook from the library.

The first year I hardly recognized the dish. I said, "Frozen lasagna would be fine, Mom. And easier, too."

"Frozen lasagna?"

"That's what Pete has. His mother heats it up in the microwave."

Mom Miller scoffed. "What a way to show

your love. Frozen lasagna heated up in the microwave."

She follows that old recipe down to the very last shake of oregano. It takes a week to make it, including going to the library, and to the grocery store, and hanging the noodles over the kitchen chairs. And every few hours she has to lie down on the sofa to rest.

Pete's mother gave her a simplified recipe one year after Pete told her how down-and-out on the sofa my mother was. But Mom Miller threw it in the wastebasket.

On the evening of July 2nd, she serves the lasagna to Pete and me out on the patio. She carries it out, steaming hot, in a huge blue pottery serving dish with sunflowers painted on the sides, and sets it in the middle of the table. Then she goes back into the house and throws a sheet over the kitchen counter and table. And she lies down on the sofa. It is the only thing that ever completely does her in.

I say to Pete on the first day of July, "It's my birthday tomorrow. Coming?"

He says, "Candles and flags and all that stuff?"

And I say, "Remember your mother's walls."

Pete's mother has cluttered walls. In an effort to preserve things, she hangs them on the walls higher than the children can reach: school papers, ribbons and awards, birthday cards, odd socks. Things that should be in scrapbooks and drawers, she tacks up on her walls. When the front door opens, the walls move. Other than that, it is an ordinary house.

"Slow down," I tell Pete out on the patio.

"Why?"

"Because Mom Miller has spent all week on this."

He nods. "Why the silver goblets?"

"Don't ask. Just slow down."

We stuff ourselves with lasagna and garlic bread, and listen to bluegrass, and give a Moose call. About an hour later Mom Miller gets up from the sofa and brings out the birthday cake.

Every year Pete starts slapping his forehead and stuttering. "N-nobody gets a birthday cake like this."

"I do. And I don't mention your mother's walls."

The cake is two feet tall, a Norwegian *kransekage*, with twenty-four rings of cake stacked up in a pyramid. White frosting drizzles down the sides and candy bonbons and tiny Norwegian flags are stuck in the frosting.

"Are you Norwegian?" Pete asks each year.

"Mr. Olsen the baker is," I tell him.

The first year Pete and I did not find the bottle of wine inside the pyramid for a couple of days. After that, we checked inside first thing. We take the bottle of wine and sit on the cool grass under a crab apple tree. And talk Norwegian:

"Yonkal ponkal Norge, ja?"

"Ja, yonkal ponkal Norge."

"Dah! Olav polav knute!"

"Dah! Feo feo fiords!"

It would take weeks for Pete and me to eat

the whole cake. So after a few days we toss the remaining rings over the handlebars of our bikes and ride out over the desert. And feed the squirrels.

That took care of my lasagna craving for one night.

Snow fell all night in the canyon, and I sat in my many sweaters and watched it. It was almost dawn when I unrolled my sleeping bag and crawled inside.

I awoke to frosted Jeep windows. I blew a peephole the size of a bagel and looked out. As I watched, a large mule deer stepped out of the trees. He stood for several minutes, turning his majestic head from side to side. Right out of *National Geographic*. And then he looked directly at me.

I could hardly breathe. The deer had survived the hunt. He had lived by my side all these weeks and had just made his presence known. We had survived together, here in Little Red Rock Canyon. I admired him. I wanted to tell him so.

I tried to roll down the window, but it was frozen shut. And so I pushed the door open and leaped out into the cold snow.

"Yonkal ponkal Norge," I cried. "Olav polav dah!"

The deer took off. Fast.

I looked down at my bare feet, turning pink in the snow. I felt like an idiot. I felt good.

12

Phillip Harkness zigzagged into the chemistry room on imaginary skis and slid into his desk. His big feet stuck out in the aisle. I caught a glimpse of pink socks and looked up with a knowing smile. I guess I stared.

"Hey, Miller," he said, leaning over. "Do you want to go skiing?"

"Skiing?" I wondered if I could risk having a friend. Just for one day. Then I thought, what the heck. "When?" I asked.

"Friday, if this keeps up," he said. "School is out for I.E.A. You know, when the Idaho

107

teachers meet—"

I nodded. "I'll see if I can get off work."

But the snow did not keep up. It melted the next day and left behind mud. The rest of the week was just like summer except most of the remaining leaves were off the trees on top of the mud.

So on Friday Phillip and I went four-wheeling in my Jeep. Tom had said I could work the late shift that day with no problem.

I picked up Phillip at his house, a redbrick bungalow a few blocks from the school. I asked him if he knew someone who could help us lift off the hardtop. It takes two men or four runts like Pete and me to lift it.

"Sure," he said. "My dad's at his shop. Why do you keep the hardtop on all the time, anyway?"

"No garage." I had unloaded my things in the scrub oak earlier that morning and hoped the critters would leave them alone. Old Maggie could take both my cowboy boots to the top of a pine tree if he wanted to.

"Just wondered," he said, and hopped inside. Phillip was a big kid who looked even bigger than usual in the front seat of my Jeep.

We drove downtown to his father's shop, Harkness Lawn and Snow Machines. Phillip went in and returned with his father. The three of us lifted that hardtop off as easy as a paper hat. I have always wanted a father who could lift a hardtop off a Jeep.

For a moment, I wondered if Mr. Joe could lift a hardtop off a Jeep. But with his sore feet, I doubted it.

Phillip's father said to leave the top right there in the driveway, and for us to have fun in the mountains. So we did.

Phillip directed the way along Foothill Road, pointing out the four canyons slicing down the mountains: Ten Mile, Five Mile, Big Red Rock. And Little Red Rock, where I lived. Of course, I did not mention that.

We stopped below a muddy mountain crowded with motorbikes and four-wheelers. "Charley's Hill," Phillip said.

"What does Charley say about all this traffic on his hill?" I asked.

"There is no Charley."

"Of course there's a Charley," I said. "A hill is not named Charley for nobody. Maybe old Charley bought this hill planning to grow Christmas trees, but"—I surveyed the frenzied scene before me—"maybe he was pushed out."

Phillip squinted his eyes. "Never thought of that."

"Mount Everest, now," I said, "the highest mountain in the world was not named Everest for nobody. It was named Everest for Sir George Everest, an Englishman, even though he never climbed it.

"And Mount Cook, over in New Zealand. It was named for Captain James Cook, another Englishman. He saw it first.

"And Mount McKinley, up in Alaska. It was named for the president of the United States, William McKinley. Now that does not mean President McKinley climbed the mountain, nor that he was the first man to see it. Some people think—"

"What do you think?" Phillip turned to face me.

What did I think? Pete would tell me I was expounding. I took a big breath of frosty air and said, "I think Charley is dead."

"Do you want to go home then?" Phillip asked.

"No," I answered. "But there is a Charley." I jumped out and locked the hubs on the front wheels.

Phillip stood up and waved his arms around. "There is a Charley. There is a Charley," he shouted. Phillip was noisy, too.

I was getting used to noisy people. I was even beginning to like them.

I climbed back in and said, "Hold on, Phillip!" And I floored it.

The Jeep crawled to the top of the hill, wheels spinning, mud flying. Then I shifted into third and we slid back down. We crawled up again and went over the top of the hill, twisting around trees and fording creeks.

Phillip was clinging to the roll bar shouting, "Man, I love this Jeep. Every year I think I might get one and guess what I get?"

"What?"

"A baby sister."

"Oh."

"I have three," he said. "What about you?"

We stopped in a shallow creek to wash the windshield so I could see to continue driving. "I have Burgess," I mumbled.

Phillip drew a smiley face on his half of the muddy windshield. "Who's Burgess?"

"Uh—uh—Burgess is my stepbrother."

"Do you take him four-wheeling?"

Four-wheeling with Burgess? "Not really," I said. "Mostly we throw each other's things out windows."

"You do that?"

"He threw mine out," I said. "Now it is my turn to throw his out. It's a thing we do."

"Man, I wish I had a brother." Phillip stared at me with some kind of admiration.

Later, driving back to camp, I thought about what Phillip had said. Maybe I would take Burgess four-wheeling—after I threw his things out the window. I had a lot of thinking to do about Burgess.

I had a lot of thinking to do about Mr. Joe. Maybe it was just his big white Cadillac with electric seatwarmers that I did not like.

That night as I lay in my sleeping bag looking out at the silver stars, I realized I had a lot of thinking to do about myself.

And I thought it is weird how sometimes friends can help you with your problems.

13

On Saturday I picked up my paycheck and then drove south of town to Home Mart, a giant discount store Mr. Flandro had recommended. Older guys know lots of useful information.

Mr. Flandro was always telling me names of stores and asking if I had enough money and enough to eat. I wondered if he would consider a boarder, in case of severe weather up the canyon.

I was slowly checking off the necessities inside my history book, although not always in order. The cell phone, for example—

In addition to food and gas, I now had toothpaste, red earmuffs, and a calendar at 75 percent off. Also a lantern as bright as a full moon. I worried about the lantern because it was shining through the bushes out to the road.

I needed black window shades.

The Home Mart's giant parking lot was crowded with cars and I had to drive around several times before I found a space. I soon saw the reason. Over the front doors a red and green banner read: CHRISTMAS IN OCTOBER. I thought it was rushing things a bit, but I went in.

Inside, the store looked like Christmas. Red and green streamers were stretched overhead and "Jingle Bells" played in the background. Shoppers pressed down the aisles, talking and laughing.

As I pushed my shopping cart I felt a sudden surge of brotherly love for all those people in the store and all those still trying to park. For the first time I felt true Moosehood, not just for Pete and me, but for all mankind. And I composed a few lines:

> *We are all family.*
> *The gray-haired man pushing his*
> *   shopping art,*
> *The child tagging after his mother,*
> *The smiling girl behind the cash register.*
> *We are all family*
> *Together.*

I pushed my cart up and down the aisles, smiling at my family of mankind and looking for the window shades. Then I began thinking about my own family, which used to be Mom Miller, Dad, and me. Then just Mom Miller and me. And now—three more people from Seattle. If I counted Mrs. Crofts.

I could not find window shades, and so I pressed my way over to the information booth and stood in line.

"For what use?" the woman asked.

"For a blackout," I said. I could not tell a total stranger about my camp life. "Like in World War II. When the enemy planes flew over, you would pull a roller shade over your window, and then when you turned on the bright light—if you had to get up in the night to go to the bathroom or to the refrigerator—the enemy pilots would not see your light. Some elderly people and babies had to—"

"You don't say."

"Every family had them," I said, "by law. Maybe they did not buy them at this store. Maybe this store was not even built then. But it was the law—"

"World War II is over," she said. "We don't have any."

A woman in the line behind me shouted, "Use garbage bags."

Other people in the line started shouting at me: "Use black shoe polish. Use anything. Just move it."

Then they started attacking the information woman: "I'm in a hurry. Where are your extension ladders? Where is your silver tinsel?"

So much for universal Moosehood. I purchased a box of black garbage bags and a roll of black duct tape and hurried out into the chilly night.

14

The paper thing glowed in front of my locker like a Halloween grin. Kids stared and snickered as they passed. Dragon waltzed over in her red high-tops.

It was impossible to avoid someone as noisy as Diantha Dragon. For two weeks I had arrived early and left late or arrived late and left early.

But she was there.

"Where did you steal that thing?" I asked.

"That thing is an authentic Chinese lantern with batteries," she said. "The old

119

geezer threw a garden party so we have a garage full. And if you wonder where I have been—I've joined the drama club. I'm rehearsing for the school play. I'm Girl Two."

I noticed Mrs. Green coming down the hall toward us. I picked up the glowing Chinese thing and shoved it into my locker.

"See you at six," Dragon called, and blew a kiss. "I'll be early."

I moved quickly and turned into my first period classroom. And there I was face-to-face with Blond Lisa. She still took my breath away.

I had rehearsed a conversation for just such a time as this, about the Masai women who shaved their heads and wore pounds and pounds of jewelry. I had read it in *National Geographic*. But all I could think of then was how good she looked in faded jeans and that white rag-wool sweater she was wearing.

So I took a deep breath and said, "Hey."

She said, "Hey," and her pink lips turned up into a little smile.

And then I said, "How do you like Red Rock?"

Her little smile changed to a kind of sneer that I hope someday to forget. "You ask me that every time," she said. "You're weird." She tossed her head and turned away.

I sank into my desk. Never again would I ask a girl a question about a town. Never again would I ask a girl a question. But a weirdo?

Then, after a while I thought, what the heck. That was enough talking to blondes for me.

After third period I hurried downstairs to the cafeteria—I was eating better now—and filled my plate with the special of the day: roast turkey and mashed potatoes. I love roast turkey and mashed potatoes.

Every Thanksgiving Mom Miller gilds a twenty-five-pound turkey with gold leaf that she orders from a specialty catalog. It takes almost as much time as the lasagna. All the school faculty drop in during the day to admire the golden masterpiece. Even Mr. and Mrs. Olsen from the bakery come.

Because of the open house, we eat late on Thanksgiving, around midnight. The year Aunt Hildy and Uncle John came, they were faint on the sofa before dinner was served.

Uncle John devoured that gold leaf just like butter. He belched and rubbed his stomach and ate more. Suddenly he stopped and whimpered in a frightened voice that gold could not be edible even if a catalog said so. He dropped back down on the sofa and declared he was poisoned.

Mom Miller called the doctor and described the symptoms. Of course Uncle John was not poisoned. He had just overeaten.

It was getting to be that time of year. So wherever in the world Mom Miller was now, I knew what she was thinking about. I did not mention the gilded turkey to the cafeteria women.

After lunch I drove fast over to the post

office. Three letters were waiting—all from Italy. I cursed Mrs. Crofts for holding my mail so long and vowed never to call her with a report again.

The first letter was a travelogue of ancient Rome: the Pantheon, which was two thousand years old and still standing; the Colosseum, half standing; and the ruins of the Roman Forum, in ruins, of course.

Mom Miller did not mention old Joe's feet, but what she did mention would detain him in Italy permanently if a blue-blooded Roman happened to overhear him. After he had walked around those old ruins all day on pinched bunions, he told Mom Miller he felt like setting a match to the place.

The last paragraph said how much she missed me and that she realized I may feel a little lonely. But she would be home before long. And to please write.

The second letter from Rome was mostly hysterical questions: "What do you mean, how is my gallbladder? What are you doing in

Red Rock, Idaho? When did Aunt Hildy and Uncle John move from Florida? Do you have money? Why don't you write? Did Burgess do something? Lester says he can be difficult. He will call and talk to him. I do hope we can all learn to get along together.

"Marty, you are my number one priority. Always number one. You know that, don't you?" And other nice things.

I wanted her to say those things and I thought I would feel better. But I felt worse. I felt guilty.

I tore open the third envelope and read the letter quickly because I was already late for chemistry. She said she had just talked to Mrs. Crofts on the telephone, who said that I called her and reported, and that I was fine at Aunt Hildy and Uncle John's. She was surprised, of course, but if that was what I wanted it was okay with her. And she would see me in Seattle soon.

Then she continued the travelogue of Rome: Michelangelo's Sistine Chapel, the

Basilica of St. Peter, and the Trevi Fountain. "Rent the old movie *Three Coins in the Fountain* and then you will see it too, Marty," she wrote.

She loved the Hotel Internazionale on a hill above the Spanish Steps where people sit and talk and write letters. That was where she was writing this. She could see Bernini's Fountain at the bottom of the steps, and on the left, the small apartment where the poet Keats died at the age of twenty-five.

"So young, Marty," she wrote, "although it may not seem young to you." She did not mention old Joe's being in jail for sabotage. Nor did she mention Thanksgiving.

I shoved all three letters into the glove compartment and returned to school. The bell had rung and the main hall was deserted. I took the glowing lantern from my locker and dropped it into the first wastebasket I passed—in front of Mrs. Green's office. She could analyze it if she wanted.

I spent a long time on my letter to Mom

Miller—through chemistry and history and in study hall—thinking what I would tell her. What I would say.

I thought about her over there in Europe with Mr. Joe, seeing all those old things, and wished she were home with me, baking pies. Rhubarb, banana cream—any kind would do.

The letter, as usual, was short:

Dear Mom Miller,
I am still intact.
How's the lasagna over there?
Your son,
Martin J. Miller

A wind had come up when I walked out to the parking lot after work. Blowing in more snow for Phillip, I hoped.

I heard a honk and looked up, just in time. Dragon's old green car almost ran over me. She stuck her head out the window and the wind whipped her hair across her face.

I stood there with my hands in my jacket

pockets looking at her without saying anything. I was not too good at saying things to
girls.

"You want me to find another boyfriend?"
she called out. "This late in the school year?
Our junior year?"

I made a great effort not to stammer. "I-I'm
your boyfriend now?"

"You're it."

I looked at her, stunned, and wondered
why I had been avoiding her, wondered if I
really liked sequins and ruffles or if I was just
getting used to the brilliance. Then I remembered.

"You're too noisy."

She leaned farther out the window and
pursed her lips together, "And you are a fanatical bore."

"Okay," I said. I shrugged and walked over
to my Jeep and climbed in. I drove out of the
parking lot feeling low-down. But a fanatical
bore? I was just trying to survive.

I drove along Foothill Road. As I turned up

Little Red Rock Canyon I glanced back and saw an old green car not far behind. My boring old spirits lifted so suddenly I felt like speeding. I stepped on the gas, then eased off, keeping one eye peering in the rearview mirror all the way up the canyon.

15

THURSDAY, NOVEMBER 8

My Jeep was turning into a regular study-
diner. Dragon and I ate lots of cold hamburgers there and read lots of world history by the
light of the propane lantern. And we talked.

"Since we are engaged—unofficially," she
said, "now what?"

I gasped out loud. "You want me to walk to
the Nevada desert, three hundred miles, and
write our names with rocks inside a heart?"

"You do that in Nevada?"

"Everyone does it. Miles and miles of
names in rock hearts on the alkali flats: Cory

loves Talia, Nate loves Emma, Randy loves Jane.

"For all the world to see."

Dragon sighed and closed her book. "They don't do things like that in Missouri," she said.

"Mom Miller sent my dad kisses from Mount Rushmore," I said. The sudden memory surprised me. My dad had told me when he was sick. I was five years old. My mom had filled in the rest later.

"They had one date—to a movie and the Red Bandanna. Then Mom Miller and her girlfriend went on a trip to Chicago and they stopped at Mount Rushmore in South Dakota to look at the presidents carved in the mountain. In the gift shop she bought a box of candy kisses and mailed it to my dad:

"RUSH MORE KISSES

TO

CHARLES L. MILLER

WINNEMUCCA, NEVADA

"When she came home, they decided to get married."

"Yeah," Dragon said, and she clapped her hands on her history book. She shimmered in the lantern light. "Mom Miller is my kind of mom."

Not really, I thought. My mother was never noisy. She did not glitter. Yet, she had sent those candy kisses. And she liked Mr. Joe's Cadillac.

I glanced across at Dragon. Not really, but—maybe I didn't know everything there was to know about Mom Miller.

The November nights were cold, but the days were warm as summer. And since no more snow had blown in for Phillip Harkness, I began riding my bike to and from school again.

One night Phillip brought his three little sisters to the Burger Box. He was tending for his parents. Mr. Flandro and I made a big fuss over the girls because they looked just alike in three different sizes. And they did not spill ketchup.

Phillip left the same time I did and he said to come on over to his place and help tend. When we walked out to the parking lot Dragon honked her car.

"Tell your girlfriend to come, too," Phillip said.

"My girlfriend?" I squinted against the setting sun.

"Sure. Isn't that Dani Dragon?"

"Oh, sure," I said.

"Lots of guys are envious." He waved for Dragon to follow.

I hopped on my bike and followed Dragon's car, my heart pounding fast. Lots of guys envious? That was new for me.

We had a good time entertaining the little sisters. Dragon performed her Girl Two part for them: entrance, three lines, and exit. It did not make sense to them, nor to Phillip and me. But we all laughed and applauded.

Phillip showed us his skis in the basement, waxed and ready for the slopes. He said to pray for snow, and we all said we would.

It was my turn next. I cupped my hands and gave a long hoarse Moose call, and they all gave Moose calls. I pronounced all five official Moose Club members. We laughed and applauded again.

Dragon danced with the little girls around and around the front room until she said she had to leave. She had play practice. We felt a bit lonely after she left.

Phillip and I took turns reading fairy tales to the girls and after a while they felt sleepy and went upstairs to bed. Then Phillip and I ate burnt almond fudge ice cream until I said it was time for me to head home.

As I pedaled up the canyon under the silver stars I shouted out old Walt's lonesome traveler lines. And I gave a couple of Moose calls. I was feeling darn good for Martin J. Miller, which is usually the time someone takes a potshot at me.

From the canyon road I saw the glow of lights through the trees and I knew someone had found my camp. I thought perhaps it was a wounded hunter or a lost hiker. I jumped from my bike and approached cautiously, and as I crept through the trampled bushes I saw the lanterns.

A string of Chinese lanterns was swinging from tree to tree, about as high as Dani Dragon could reach on her toes. Those lanterns were exposing my camp to the whole world.

In a rage I pulled them down and stomped on them. I jumped and kicked until they were broken shards in the dirt.

The little critters were unusually silent.

I stared into the darkness and slowly the dreadful reality sank in. My Jeep was gone.

"Dragon?" I called.

Of course she was not there. She had strung the lights as a surprise. Someone had seen the lights from the road, and then my Jeep. Someone who wanted to go four-wheeling, desperately—or to Mexico.

My things were scattered around the camp and I stumbled over them in the darkness. I shouted out curses. Finally I gathered up some of my clothes and dragged them into the scrub oak. I lay down and pulled a sweater over my head.

I was homeless.

The next morning I was late for school. I suspected everyone who looked at me—Dragon, Phillip, Mr. Fields, Mrs. Green. And those who did not—Lisa, Patty, Kate, and Sammy, and five hundred other Woodland Rams.

At noon Dragon followed me to the front entrance. "How did you like—"

"I didn't like it," I scowled. "And in case you don't know, my Jeep has been stolen."

She let out a little cry. "I am so sorry, Marty," she said. "I was just thinking to surprise you. Sometimes you are so—"

"Boring?" I grabbed her arm and we walked out of school and around to the back door. We sat on the steps.

"This is a talk," I said. I could not look at

her and I was having trouble breathing.

We sat in silence listening to each other breathe, and then I mumbled, "And something else—I'm temporary." I looked at her then.

"I know that," she said in a soft whisper.

"Just so you know."

She stood up. "Now what can we do about the Jeep?"

"The first thing," I said, "is to look around Charley's Hill. You could drive me up the canyon and we'll see if anyone is on the hill with it."

"Okay," she said. "Let's go now."

We drove up Big Red Rock Canyon to Charley's Hill and looked around. We saw a few motorbikes, but no Jeeps. We drove up the other three canyons, looking. Then it was time for me to go to work.

"Let's go to the police, Marty," Dragon said.

"Not yet," I said. "Just drop me off at work."

When I walked into the Burger Box, Mr. Flandro looked up, "What's the problem,

Marty? Maybe I can help."

I pulled on the paper hat and tied the red-and-white checked apron slowly, thinking I would like to tell Mr. Flandro, just as I would tell my dad. But I also knew Mr. Flandro would want to do the adult thing—call the police. And the police would have a few questions to ask me.

So I said, "It's midterm week. But thanks anyway, Mr. Flandro."

After work I rode my bike to Phillip's house. Since he knew all the kids at school, I thought he might have heard something.

Phillip answered the door and we went down to the basement to talk. I was only going to tell him about my missing Jeep, but once I got started, I told him all about Winnemucca and Mom Miller. Pete. Mr. Olsen the baker. Miss Addison. Mr. Joe Wonderful and Burgess. Baggy Legs. I did not leave anyone out.

When I finished he said, "I wish I had an old Jeep."

Phillip wanted to ask his dad for advice,

but we both knew what Mr. Harkness would do, the same as Mr. Flandro. We decided to handle it ourselves.

Phillip asked where I was sleeping and when I told him in a bush, he said I could stay at his house. I could sleep on the sofa right where I was sitting. And he said, "Don't worry too much about your Jeep. We will find it. I know my Rocky Mountains."

For a long time I lay on the sofa looking up at the ceiling, unable to sleep. I did not like temporary. I wanted to go home. I knew home was not in a sleeping bag in the back of my Jeep. And it was not on a lumpy plaid sofa in a friend's basement.

I thought about all the people I knew in Red Rock, all the people in Winnemucca, and the ones in Seattle.

And I knew in my heart that if Mom Miller lived on upper Ivy Cliff Drive in Seattle, that was my home, too.

16

Before the sun made it over the mountains on Saturday, Phillip, Dragon, and I drove up Big Red Rock Canyon and up Charley's Hill as far as the old Chevrolet would go. We parked the sputtering car next to an old gnarled juniper and started walking. We were the only ones on the hill.

Phillip led the way because, as he said, he knows his Rocky Mountains. Dragon and I followed. I carried a gallon can of gas, just in case, and Dragon fluttered along, her silver bracelets jingling.

We walked to the top of the hill, down the other side, and up another hill. Then we followed a narrow dirt road that criss-crossed a shallow creek. There were many Jeep tracks.

"I love these mountains," Phillip shouted over and over again. He waved his arms around as if he were hugging them. "I love them in the summer, I love them in the fall, I love them in the winter—"

I trudged along behind Phillip with the gas can bumping against my leg. I changed it to the other side and kept walking and looking. And thinking hard about life. And about my unknown enemy.

Hours later we stopped because a large boulder blocked the road. We leaned against it to rest.

I dropped the gas can in the shade of the rock. "I don't think my Jeep is in the mountains."

"I guess not," Phillip said. "I guess it wasn't kids who took it."

"I am really sorry," Dragon said. She

brushed bits of dirt and leaves from her yellow ruffle.

I thought if I heard those bracelets jingle one more time— "Have you ever heard of the Masai women?" I asked.

"Who?"

"The Masai women. They wear a lot of jewelry."

"All women wear jewelry."

"Not like the Masai."

"Is it something you read in *National Geographic*?" she asked.

I did not answer.

We lay back on the boulder and watched two hawks circling in the pale sky above us. That is, Phillip and Dragon watched the hawks. I could only think of my Jeep and the person who took it.

Oh, I had enemies. I made a mental list of all of them, living and dead:

Jeep thief
Baggy Legs
Mrs. Green

U.S. postal clerk
Blond Lisa
Unknown number of customers at Home Mart

I had enemies, all right:

Hitler
Attila the Hun
The bloody Philistines

I decided I had more enemies than friends and probably always would have. So—

Dragon nudged me with her elbow. "So now what?"

"Those Masai women wear pounds and pounds of jewelry—copper wire earrings as big as steering wheels—"

Phillip sat up. "I think we should contact the police."

"Okay," I said.

"Let's run," Dragon said.

Phillip and Dragon took off running. The gas can slowed me down.

• • •

At the bottom of the canyon on Foothill Road I asked Dragon to pull over at the post office. I needed to make a phone call.

Mrs. Crofts answered and she was unusually chatty. She said Mom Miller and Mr. Joe would be home four days before Thanksgiving. My mother had mentioned something about needing time to gild a turkey, but Mrs. Crofts did not understand it. And she wondered if I would be home.

"Plan on me." Then I said, "Tell Burgess"— I took a deep breath—"tell Burgess to secure his belongings."

"What?" Mrs. Crofts asked, no longer chatty. "Tell him what?"

"I can't hear you, Mrs. Crofts, over the static."

"What static?"

"I can't hear you, Mrs. Crofts."

We stopped at the police station downtown. It looked a lot like a jail to me and my legs felt weak walking up to the front door. Phillip and Dragon walked on either side.

I filled out a report with my name, Phillip's address and Phillip's phone number, and a description of my Jeep. And place of theft: Little Red Rock Canyon.

The sergeant had no information on stolen Jeeps. He dropped my report into a file. No one in the Red Rock Police Department cared much about me or my old red Jeep.

Later, as I was lying awake on the plaid sofa, I started thinking about the list I had made. And I thought maybe I could start a list of friends, a short but meaningful list:

Diantha Dragon
Phillip Harkness
Pete
Moses

And who knows? Someday I might have more.

17

I pulled out of Red Rock, Idaho, on a cold November afternoon in three inches of snow, sitting third seat on the right in a Greyhound bus. My mountain bike was stashed in the luggage compartment underneath. Mrs. Harkness had invited me to stay for Thanksgiving, but I said I could not miss my mother's gilded turkey.

"Gilded turkey?"

"It's just an adjective." I did not want to tell anybody's mother about our turkey. I never knew when to stop.

But Mrs. Harkness had let me sleep on her plaid sofa for a week. I would send her a catalog and a color picture after I arrived home. And I would add her name to my list of friends.

I made a few stops on my bike before leaving town. First I checked at the police station as I had each morning for over a week. The sergeant on duty shook his head when he saw me. Jeeps never turn up.

I jumped back on my bike and pedaled like a madman. I wanted my Jeep. I wanted to go home in my Jeep.

Then because it was too early to go anywhere else, I headed for Little Red Rock Canyon. The road was snow-packed, but I could see from the tracks that a four-wheeler had gone up. I pedaled behind in the narrow path.

My Camp of Many Critters was covered with snow and I did not want to disturb it. I stood just inside the bush gate and repeated my Camp Oath: I will never bring disgrace on this my Camp of Many Critters. I will not litter . . . I will not trample. . . .

Being human, I had trampled. I had littered. And I had rearranged a few rocks. But there was no sign that I had ever been there. And whatever litter was under the layer of snow, Maggie would take care of for me.

As I turned to leave I heard a fluttering of wings. Maggie flew down to a low branch near my head and started to sing. And then all the little critters joined in—cawing, chirping, squealing, trilling.

Feeling about as good as Martin J. Miller can feel, I tiptoed out of my Camp of Many Critters.

At the Burger Box I stopped to give my resignation to Tom and Mr. Flandro. Tom nodded as he cleaned the grill, but Mr. Flandro came around the counter in his apron and said to sit down and take off my wet shoes. I told him a simplified version of my life history so he would understand my reason for leaving.

He said he understood. He gave me a sack

of warm hamburgers for the trip and said I could always come back for a summer job.

At the door I glanced up at the sign on top of the red-and-white pole. I turned back. "A suggestion," I said. "Burgers So Good You'll Wanna Have More."

Mr. Flandro and Tom smiled and nodded. I would miss them both.

I ate the hamburgers on the way to Woodland High to check on my fees.

"Fees for three months?" Mrs. Green looked up from her desk, nervous still.

"Just round it out."

I stacked my six textbooks on her desk. Inside my history book I had checked off most of my necessities: earmuffs, reading lamp, calendar, toothpaste—

"Is this everything?" Mrs. Green asked.

"Everything except ice cubes, cell phone, and"—I sighed—"but they can wait."

With a flourish Mrs. Green checked off my name on the absentee list. I noticed on top of the list another name, Diantha Dragon.

I found Dragon's address in the school directory and rode my bike to her house—a house with lots of windows—on the foothills east of town. I was surprised I had not noticed it before.

I leaned my bike against a tree, walked up to the front door, and rang the doorbell.

An older man answered. His shirt was buttoned to the very top button. "Yes?" he said.

I asked for Dragon and he said to come in and sit down.

I sat on a white sofa and looked around. Zebra rug. Black grand piano. Trees in pots. And overhead, a hanging metal sculpture—rings and rods, balls and stars. This was a classy place.

I was still staring at the ceiling when Dragon appeared. She was wearing all black, with silver bracelets jingling on her arm. She sat down on another white sofa across from me and leaned forward expectantly.

"Kinetic movement," I said. "Mr. Fields would love it."

I am not very good at farewells and I knew I was not doing very well with this one. I looked away from the mobile.

"Is this another talk?" she asked.

"It's another talk."

"Then is our engagement officially off?" she asked.

"For the present, I guess."

"Then I shall wear black until the day I die."

"You already do that," I said, "wear black." She rose tremulously and steadied herself against the arm of the sofa. She was going to be great in the school play. I stood, and we walked toward the door.

Outside, she said, "You're not such a fanatical bore as you once were, Marty."

I smiled. "And you're not so noisy, Dragon," I said.

I looked at my watch. "The G-Greyhound bus leaves in half an hour," I stammered. I am not very good at farewells, as I mentioned.

"So do we kiss now?" Right there in full view of all Red Rock, she said that.

So we kissed. I was feeling sad, feeling that if I left Diantha Dragon on this doorstep I would never see her again.

But you never know.

She was still standing on her doorstep, waving, when I rode away on my bike. Glittering and noisy. I wonder if I will love her forever.

That old Greyhound bus was slow-moving, so slow I thought the driver had dozed off at the wheel. I watched the back of his motionless head for as long as I could stand it and then I jumped up and shouted, "Hey."

His head jerked up then and he looked back through the rearview mirror.

While I was up I looked around at my family of mankind—a few elderly women with blue-gray hair and a few men who looked a lot like Baggy Legs. They stared blankly at me—those who were awake. One man wearing a bandanna around his head lifted his right hand and said, "Here." The woman across the aisle smiled and nodded.

I wondered where they were headed. I wondered if they were all going to Seattle and if I should invite them home to see the turkey.

I dropped back down in my seat and held my hands over my face. I had visions of my Jeep, mud-splashed and smeared with ketchup, somewhere south in Las Vegas or Tijuana. I punched the seat in front a few times and kicked the footrests.

I don't like Greyhound buses.

I began fiddling around with the window, trying to open it, but discovered it was sealed shut. Then I discovered I was not breathing and I jumped up again. I did not intend to expire on a Greyhound bus.

I sat back down and stared out the window.

In the frosted fields black-and-white cows grazed on scattered bales of hay. And bales of hay were piled high into stacks. Miles and miles of haystacks.

In a corner of one field three bales were stacked one on top of the other. A large red heart was painted on the side, with the message: ERIC LOVES KATE.

In the next field was another stack of bales: STUART LOVES JADA.

So that's what they do in Idaho. I thought of Dragon and smiled. The woman across the aisle smiled and nodded again.

Later, after dark, I composed a few lines about the black-and-white cows and recited them against the sealed window:

The cows in the pasture, black-and-white,
The cows in the pasture grazing,
Beautiful, these kindly cows,
Chewing on hay bales, contented.

Then I started wondering if those cows were the same cows I had seen when I had traveled in the opposite direction three months earlier when I had been hungry, homeless, and sweating in my old red Jeep.

Then I decided, what the heck. I was not
even the same person I was then. No one in
Winnemucca would recognize me now without my Jeep. Not Miss Addison, not Pete, not
Leo Burnette. Like old Walt, I had walked
that lonesome valley. I had walked it by
myself.

Now I was going home.

Not home to Winnemucca, Nevada, just
off Main Street where my heart would always
be, but home to upper Ivy Cliff Drive in
Seattle where grass grows.

And it was okay with me for now to let it
grow.